AF406833

LEXI RICHARDS

Becoming Greyson: Greyson Girls Prequel

First published by Ladyalex Productions 2022

Copyright © 2022 by Lexi Richards

All rights reserved. No part of this publication may be reproduced, stored or transmitted in any form or by any means, electronic, mechanical, photocopying, recording, scanning, or otherwise without written permission from the publisher. It is illegal to copy this book, post it to a website, or distribute it by any other means without permission.

This novel is entirely a work of fiction. The names, characters and incidents portrayed in it are the work of the author's imagination. Any resemblance to actual persons, living or dead, events or localities is entirely coincidental.

Lexi Richards asserts the moral right to be identified as the author of this work.

Lexi Richards has no responsibility for the persistence or accuracy of URLs for external or third-party Internet Websites referred to in this publication and does not guarantee that any content on such Websites is, or will remain, accurate or appropriate.

Designations used by companies to distinguish their products are often claimed as trademarks. All brand names and product names used in this book and on its cover are trade names, service marks, trademarks and registered trademarks of their respective owners. The publishers and the book are not associated with any product or vendor mentioned in this book. None of the companies referenced within the book have endorsed the book.

First edition

This book was professionally typeset on Reedsy.
Find out more at reedsy.com

Contents

Chapter 1

My name is Alexandra Hart, and I've done nothing useful with my life in all of my 23 years. I've never even been to college because I'm broke and spend the majority of my small income on my small apartment. My family isn't what you would exactly call a 'family,' either. You see, my parents separated when I was pretty young. My mother decided that she didn't want to be a mother or wife anymore and just left. Left without looking back once. Like her whole family was a distant memory that she wished she could bury deep down. I never understood how a mother could walk out on her family like that. Since the day she left, we haven't heard a thing. I guess she doesn't care. The day after I graduated, I told my dad was going to try out living out on my own. I had already saved up enough to keep myself comfortable for a couple of months, and I knew I could manage with my working hours.

My dad has always trusted me and always respected my desires and wishes. He didn't even try and argue with me. He's been my rock since I was a kid, and he's always kept me steady on my feet. I will always respect my father for taking on the role of mom and dad. I sometimes hate my mom for putting him through that, but I know he doesn't hate her, so I try not to. On my 15th birthday, my dad surprised me with my cat Finn. I had been begging him for a cat for years before he finally let up. Finn has been my best friend, and I don't know what I would do without him. He knows me more than anyone, and he doesn't even know it. There have been so many nights where I would just lay across my bed and talk to him. He loved sleeping on the foot of my bed, and I always enjoyed the constant company. My life is honestly not very interesting. I basically hang out with Finn and work.

My whole life consists of work, work, work, and… Oh yeah, work. I work at a small coffee shop, Forever Cafe. Fortunately, it's down the street, a couple of blocks from where I live. I got really lucky to be hired. I don't make much, but it's enough to survive, and sometimes I get great tips! My life is also very unstable. I can't remember the last time I didn't just feel worried. That voice in my head tells me I'll always feel lost. I often daydream about what it would be like to have a perfect family with a mom who cooked dinner for me every night or calls me to tell me she misses me. I wonder what it would be like to have money or what it even feels like to be stable. I mean, the rent's paid, but I don't have room for a lot of extras. I find myself wishing for a taste of the things I think about daily. Before I knew it, Life got harder. I felt completely worn down all of the time, and I started losing hope of ever feeling happy. That is until I met him. The man who unexpectedly gave me hope and who taught me what it means to love with all of your soul. He showed me a love that was passionate and beautiful. The man who completely caught me off guard and made me fall in love with him before I could even stop myself. My eyes snap open, and I realize that my alarm hasn't gone off. I clumsily reach for my phone, knocking over loose items on my nightstand in the process.

I groan as the screen lights up and shows me that it's 8:26 AM. I am running 30 minutes late. Again. I did this last week as well. I mentally slap myself for being so irresponsible. I hastily throw the covers off in a panic making Finn hop off the bed and duck under a chair in the corner of my room. "Not again. Not again." I mutter as I peel off the baggy shirt I am wearing. I grab my uniform for work off of the pile of clean laundry that desperately needs to be folded. I pull the dark blue polo over my head and yank my simple black pants on. I pick up the pile of clothes and throw them on the floor of my closet. Staying on top of the chores was almost impossible with the amount of work I had been doing this past month. Honestly, I like it, though. I like working all of the time because it keeps me distracted from my thoughts. It keeps me out of my empty house and forces me to socialize. I needed this job, and I love it. I go into my bathroom and try my best to make it look as if I'm not completely exhausted.

After running a brush through the shaggy bead head, I pull the light strands into a messy braid and secure it in place with a hair tie. I look at my reflection in the mirror, and all I see are my tired grayish-green eyes. I let out a long sigh. Today was going to be a long one. I lock up the apartment and make my way down to Forever Cafe, my home away from home; it seems at times. I check the time. I have 20 minutes to spare. There was no way I would be late again, so I pick up my speed.

Chapter 2

When I finally reached the shop, I am out of breath. I look at the clock one more time and let out a happy sigh, "Nice. Right on time!" I walk through the doors with my head held high. I decided on my way to work that I would make today a good one, even though I am exhausted as hell. I clock in and throw on my apron. I walk to the front by the cash register. I greet customers as they come in and even attempt to throw a smile on my face so that I don't scare them off.

There was a small laugh behind me and a "hey, Alli!" I quickly glance over my shoulder. Jessica, my coworker, and best friend, has just arrived for her shift. Working with my best friend is the best thing in the world. We have a really special bond, and she understands me completely. I watch as she effortlessly throws her bright red hair into a huge messy bun on the top of her head. I wish I had her confidence. She grins at me and grabs an apron that hangs on one of the hooks.

"I'm assuming your alarm didn't go off?" She raises her

eyebrows at my messy braid and tired eyes.

"This wouldn't be the first time." rolling my eyes. We both laugh and get to work.

The day drags on slowly, but it isn't horrible. The customers have all been friendly today, and it puts me in a good mood. I glance at the clock on the wall in front of me and realize it's my break time. I walk to the back of the shop and sit down in a random chair. I close my eyes, and it feels so good. Even though today has been going great, I still feel a headache coming on. I close my eyes and groan while rubbing my temples. Jeez, I need some sleep. When my shift ends, I hang up my apron and wave goodbye to Jess.

"Love you!'" She yells obnoxiously loud as she leaves.

I yell back, "I love you," grab my coffee and bag off of the counter, and head for the exit. I could not wait to get home and take a long nap. My phone dings in my pocket, and I look down to check it. Before I look back up, I collide with something hard. My mouth opens in a mild shout as I watch my coffee fly from my hand onto a very well-dressed man.

He is wearing a light gray suit, and unfortunately, it looks expensive. Feeling embarrassed, I avoid looking at his face and begin rubbing at one of the stains with some napkins I was holding. "Oh my gosh! I am so sorry! I wasn't watching where I was going; it was a complete accident. Oh gosh, this is going to stain. I have a tendency to word vomit when I'm nervous. Jess calls it verbal diarrhea but potato potahto.

I am interrupted as two strong hands grab onto my wrists and stop my frantic rubbing. I blink slowly and look up. I was pretty sure at that moment I forget how to breathe

The man standing before me looks like he belongs on a magazine cover. He has the kind of face that makes you stop and look twice without thinking about it. He towers over me, and without thinking, I wish he would let go of my wrists so that I could take a step back and take all of him in.

My eyes flicker up to his, and I am met with searing dark blue eyes. I quickly look down, feeling panic start to form inside of me. His hand is still around my wrists! How could you be so stupid and not watch where you're going? Why are you always so clumsy? My inner tirade is interrupted.

"Did you not hear me?" His voice rings in my ears. It's quiet, deep, and husky. I am shocked at how much I want him to keep talking.

"Huh?" I say stupidly, snapping myself out of my thoughts. Why am I acting like this? I must look like a complete moron. I dare to meet his eyes again; he looks even more pissed than he did a second ago. Yup, I looked like a moron for sure.

"How careless can you be! Look at this shit." His grip tightens on my wrists before he drops them in disgust. I wince at his harsh words and stumble back in complete shock. What the hell was wrong with this guy

"I will pay for the damages, of course," I say a little too quietly. I hate to admit it, but I'm intimated and caught off guard by how he is affecting me.

He laughs loudly, which makes my eyes widen in shock. Why the heck was he laughing? He looks me up and down, and my knees feel like they might turn to Jell-O. "You?! You?!" He laughs even louder, causing people at nearby tables to glance over.

"Umm. well, I don't get paid until next week, but I can pay for the damages when I get that, no problem at all. I'll even give you my number so that I can find a way to get it to you."

He stops laughing, and his expression goes from amused to

ice-cold. "A girl like you could never afford even a piece of this fabric. Let me ask you something. How much do you think this cost me?" He gestures to his dark suit jacket.

I give him a puzzled look. What was this guy going on about? Why couldn't he just let it go? "Um, $100 or $200, maybe?" I'm praying it's not more than that. Even $100 would set me back, and I would have to work more shifts to cover the loss.

He sneers at me and crosses his arms over his chest. "You want to times that by ten?"

My mouth drops open, and I swear I see a slight look of amusement on his face. My voice comes out as barely a whisper, "T-that much?"

"Oh yeah, angel. That much. Now… how are you going to pay me back?"

Chapter 3

His eyes slowly trail down my body, and I feel naked under his intense stare. I clear my throat and ignore the butterflies beginning to form in my stomach after he called me "angel." Despite how much he is affecting me, I am livid. How dare this asshole speak to me like I'm garbage. It's just a damn suit! I gather my nerves and look him square in the eyes. Handsome bastard. Get ahold of yourself, Alli. This one is a grade-A jerk face.

He slowly taps his foot on the ground as if waiting for me to respond. I want to slap that stupid smirk right off of his perfect face. Before I can stop myself, the words start falling out of my mouth. "Who in the hell do you think you are?! You can't just treat people like shit! My life is already tough enough without you making it harder! I don't need some rude bastard like you making me feel worthless because I'm not well off. If you think you can just come in here and act like a child about a stupid stain on your damn suit, then you CLEARLY need some help!"

I rip open my bag and riffle through it to pull out my wallet.

He watches me with a shocked expression on his face as I dig through it quickly, pulling out a $20 and about 7 or 8 one-dollar bills, and I throw them at his face. Shit!! Abort! Abort! What in the name of all that is holy did I do? I hope and pray Ian didn't see that, or I am so fired. I've got to get the hell out of here. Now.

I shove past blue eyes and practically run out of the coffee shop. I step out onto the street and glance over my shoulder to see if he is following me. I feel satisfied when I see his face is still frozen in shock. He turns toward my direction, and his eyes lock on mine. I flip him off and quickly duck around a corner in case he gets any crazy ideas about following me. I do not need some lunatic chasing after me, even if he is the most attractive man I've ever seen. I can't believe I decided to antagonize him more by flipping him off, but so what? He's a jerk, and I was pissed off.

I can't believe I was stupid enough to shove my tip money in his face. I worked hard for that. Damn him. Today was steady, but no great tippers. I had mostly college kids, so I understand. Dangit, I needed that money. It's all his fault. Yes, I'm the one that threw it, but he deserved it. No money for the rainy day fund tonight. Not smart, Alli girl. Not smart at all. Did I really word vomit on someone after ruining his clothes and feeling him up? Then I threw cash in his face. Oh well, no use in crying over spilled cash. Next time, I'll hit him with coins. A big ole bag of nickels, I chuckle to myself. The chest was nice, though.

When I finally reach the door of my apartment, I let out a sigh of relief. This day turned so quickly. I'm so exhausted I feel like I might puke any second. I unlock the rusty lock and push my way into my small apartment. Home not so sweet home. Finn is waiting by the door for me like he usually is and rubs himself against my leg, purring loudly. He's the bright spot of my day. "Hey, buddy. Hope your day was better than mine." I scratch his soft orange fur, and I already feel a little bit better. I throw my bag down and flop onto my bed. I am too overwhelmed and exhausted to change out of my clothes. I lay in bed for about an hour without any sign of sleep.

I check the time. It reads 11:11 p.m. My dad used to tell me as a kid that this was the wishing hour, and I could make any wish I wanted. He told me if I wished hard enough, it might come true. I still find myself doing it even though I'm an adult. I know that making wishes is just a silly game, yet, it comforts me, so I have continued to do it. I close my eyes and hope that maybe wishes do come true and that man will go away like a puff of smoke and never bother me again. Please, I will take back every other wish I have made if you ensure I never have to run into that jerk again. Let me wake up and forget this day ever happened.

Finn nestles up to me, purring loudly. I can't help but smile despite everything that's happened today. I pull the covers up higher and close my eyes, wishing for sleep to find its way to me.

Instead, I toss and turn. I can't get those piercing blue eyes out of my mind. The body of an Adonis and a face that is so beautiful it would make anyone speechless. And I was. I looked like an idiot until he pissed me off.

Stupid jerk!

Okay, so I ruined his $2000 suit.

Obviously, he can afford it.

Why did he have to be such an asshole and look so damned good while doing it?

Argh! I need to stop thinking about Adonis and get some

sleep.

I nuzzled closer to Finn and finally drifted off to sleep with thoughts of dazzling blue eyes dancing through my mind.

Chapter 4

Maximilian

I'm intrigued that a small girl like her would stand up for herself and go so far as to throw money at me. I haven't been able to get her off of my mind. I can't help it—I'm drawn to how she stands up for herself, even when it means throwing money in my face. The way she doesn't care about how I look. I'm not being arrogant. I know I'm a catch. Handsome, fit, and rich. I'm the total package.

And then there's the fact that she's so small…

I know that I was a rude and condescending asshole. Maybe if I apologize, she'll give me the chance to make it up to her. It's not her fault I was already angry and looking for an outlet. It's not fair that she bore the brunt of something she had nothing to do with.

I go back to the same coffee shop the next day, hoping to see her and apologize.

Simon and I had been in negotiations with a European company for weeks, and just as we were about to close the deal, they tried to change it. Sadie Lugoff thought she could get a rich husband out of the deal and sweet-talked her daddy into suggesting a 'merger.' Neither of us cared whose idea it was. It's complete bullshit, and we don't do business that way. I'd just gotten off the phone with Lugoff and told him in no uncertain terms that he could go fuck himself. Even if he came back to the table begging, we would not be doing any business with him. His company was failing, and thanks to his stupidity or greed, he'll have to look elsewhere for a buyer.

The collision with the tiny warrior might have been equally my fault. The flash of anger in her odd-colored eyes made my dick immediately jump to attention. I wanted to diffuse the situation and see if she'd let me get to know her better, but I acted like an ass instead, and I'm glad she called me on it. I couldn't help myself. I was so turned on by her fire. I had to see what she'd do. Sick, I know. She did not disappoint.

She has a bigger pair of lady balls than a lot of the men I know. Maybe one day, she'll let me see them up close and personal. Woah, Maxum, we don't want to see any balls unless they're attached below. However, I wouldn't mind seeing what she had in those tight black slacks. They covered what I'm sure is a very nice ass. Round, plump and tight. I couldn't help but watch it as she stormed away from me. Then the little spitfire flipped me off. I fucking loved it! Yes. I can't wait to get to know her much better.

As I walk in, I don't see her. I walk up to the counter, order my usual (a Caffe Americano and a shot of espresso on the side) and sit down at a table near where she threw money at me yesterday. I'm hoping that she will turn up once more. I want to know if the pull I felt for her is real or if it was residual from already being full of adrenaline. I boot up my laptop and decide to get some work done while I wait for the tiny warrior. I chuckle. Somehow, I know she's going to give me hell for calling her that. I work for a couple of hours. She's still not here, and it looks as if today is going to be a bust. I need to find her. I want her. It's as simple as that.

I'm not big on social media, but I wonder…

I am glancing at some profile pictures. I pull up Forever Cafe's site and scan their photos. I scan some profiles and watch life play out before me, and just when I'm about to give up bam! Alli Hart. I wonder if that's her real name. I gather my courage and an espresso shot and open the messenger app on my phone. I type out the one phrase that I always use when I am in a sad mood:

I wonder if she'll respond.

One minute goes by. Two minutes. Three minutes. First, I'm anxious to see if she's going to come to the coffee shop for me to apologize. Now, I'm scared to see if there is going to be an answer to my instant message. I'm in deep. I can feel it. My papa told me he knew mom was the one the moment he laid eyes on her. I know the feeling. It's the Greyson way. We know what we want, and we go after it.

Eventually, a half hour passes, and it takes all of my restraint not to take this phone and smash it against the wall. My nerves are shot — but maybe that's due to the insane amount of caffeine I've consumed in the past thirty minutes. I'll cut back at some point but today's not the day.

She's a no-show, but the battle is not over. I'll be back, my tiny warrior. Enjoy your reprieve, little one. We've only just begun.

I get up, pay for my drink, and whistle a tune as I start walking toward the subway.

Alli

I wake up feeling just as exhausted as I felt when I finally drifted off to sleep last night. Today is my day off, and I immediately feel very thankful because I am struggling to get out of bed this morning. My eyes find their way to the fan circulating above me. My thoughts begin to drift to the awful scene that happened yesterday at the coffee shop. I feel my face heat up and roll over with a groan. I grab my phone off of the nightstand and check the time. 9:00 a.m. My phone lets out a loud ringing sound, and I nearly drop it. I check the caller ID and see that my dad is calling. I smile and immediately answer.

"Hey, Dad! What's up?" I ask, clearing my throat. I can practically hear him smiling as he responds in a cheerful voice, "Hey, sweetie! Sorry if I woke you, but I want you to come down and have some lunch with me at our favorite spot. Around noon. Aren't you off today? I have someone that I want to talk to you about."

I run my hands through my hair, and the corners of my mouth

lift. "Dad, I'm so happy for you. I was hoping you would meet someone when I left. I'm excited to find out who this mystery lady is!"

He must've been holding his breath because he lets out a big sigh, "I am so glad, honey. I don't know why I was so nervous to tell you. It's not like I've made a move or anything" My poor dad always worried about everyone else except himself. I assure him that I will be at Susie's Diner at noon and hang up. I set my phone down and start to get ready for the day.

At 11:30 am, I am ready to go. I check my appearance in the mirror and feel satisfied with how I look. I kept it simple and threw on my favorite light blue blouse, small white flowers etched into the collar line, and my favorite pair of jeans. I leave my hair down because it looks decent enough as it is, grab my bag, and say goodbye to Finn. He looks up from the corner of my bed, stretches out, and immediately curls back up into a ball, falling asleep. You lucky cat!

When I reach the diner, I spot my dad in the window, sitting at our usual table. We consistently came to this diner every Saturday night for years and got the same order of burgers and fries. Unfortunately, it's been weeks since we've eaten here together because of my busy work schedule. I feel sad thinking about our tradition being broken so often. My dad looks out the window as if he knows I'm there and starts waving at me when he sees me. I wave back and wipe the corner of my eye before heading in. The host guides me over to the table smiling brightly. Hmm. She must be new because I'd never seen her before.

My dad and I catch up and immediately ease into our usual banter. I almost forget that he told me he would be telling me about his mystery lady when our server Debbie walks over with a huge grin. Debbie is very beautiful, and you wouldn't think she was anywhere near her early 50s. My dad and I have known Debbie for years. She's always worked at this diner, and she's always been our server.

"Hey, Deb!" My dad said in his usual cheerful voice. Deb? Hold on a second… I look at my dad, and his face is flushed. Okay, either my dad is getting sick, or something is going on here. Debbie looks down at my dad, and I swear there's electricity that wasn't there a second ago. She breaks eye contact after a couple of seconds, and my dad loudly clears his throat. He immediately hides his face behind the menu, which is odd, considering we get the same thing every time. Debby breaks the awkward silence by turning to me, "How are you, Alli? I feel like it's been ages since we've seen you here! I know your dad has been missing you."

Debbie and I briefly catch up, but my dad is still hidden behind the menu. "Do I just bring out the usual for you two?" I nod and hand her my menu. My dad hands over his, and I swear I catch him winking at her. She tucks her brown hair behind her ear and walks away, blushing. Who would've thought? Debbie and my dad might try and deny it, but it's so obvious what's going on here.

"So… Debbie, huh?" My dad chokes on his water and goes into a coughing fit. I know the expression on my face is full of amusement, but I can't help it. He is being so weird about this.

"Is it that obvious?" He asks after he is finished coughing. I nod my head and grin.

"So, how long have you two been seeing each other?"

His faces go red, and he scratches the back of his head nervously. "Well, we haven't gone out or anything"

My eyes widen, "Why not? It's about time you started dating

again, dad! Plus, it's obvious that you two like each other" My dad bites his fingernails and shakes his head as if he's unsure what to say. Sometimes my dad can be the biggest chicken. "Dad! This could be your only chance at finding real love again. Don't you miss having someone to love?"

My dad looks up at me, and his eyes soften. He seems to be searching my face as if trying to figure something out. Surprising me, he balls his hands into fists and grins so wide that the lines on his face stand out. "You're uhh, right, baby girl! I need to do this." Uh oh. I have no idea what he means by that. Debbie walks back over to our table, this time with our food in her hands as if on cue. She places our plates, loaded with burgers and fries, down on the table. "Well, here you go, sweethearts. Can I get you anything else?"

I start to shake my head and thank her when my dad suddenly stands up, his face still red. He turns to face Debbie and grabs both of her hands. "Deb, I think you are the most beautiful woman I've ever laid eyes on. I should've done these ages ago. Will you do me the honor of going on a date with me?" My mouth drops open, and I feel a bit uncomfortable as people start to turn in their seats to see what's going on.

Debbie's eyes widen, and she says nothing as if she's in shock. I think she might be redder than my dad is. She doesn't say anything for a long moment, and I'm afraid she's about to reject him, but she smiles instead and hugs him. "W-well, I mean, of course, I will! It took you long enough!" Loud clapping rings out all around us. I clap along with them and smile at my dad. He beams at Debbie and kisses her cheek. Debbie starts giggling and shoves at his shoulder playfully. I shove a fry in my mouth, look out the window, and sigh. Must be nice to experience something like that.

Chapter 6

My dad walks me out to my car and pulls me in for a hug. I close my eyes and instantly relax. I needed today so badly. "Thanks again, baby girl" He pulls back and ruffles up my hair.

I laugh at his playful gesture and smoothed my hair back down. "It was nothing, dad. All you needed was a little push."

He laughs and runs a hand through his dark-cropped hair. My dad and I look a lot alike, and I love that. I got my hair from the incubator, but the rest is all dad. He looks me over and says suddenly, "what about you?"

Puzzled, I ask, "what about me?"

"When are you going to start dating? You are a grown woman now, and I think it would be good for you to find someone. Someone who can support and love you as much as your dear old dad does."

I burst out laughing, "good one, dad!"

My dad's face becomes serious, "honey, I mean it. When are you going to start trusting someone other than me? You will never be happy if you are always afraid to trust."

I bite my lip and look away, almost embarrassed. Memories of my father crying alone in his room at night and trying to hide it the following day with a smile flashed in my mind. My mother abandoned my father and me when I was in elementary school. Dad was utterly heartbroken. I was hurt and confused when she left, and I still had difficulty understanding why. After going through all that, I've learned that relying on others won't get you anywhere except hurt. If my mother couldn't stick around, why would anyone else? Honestly, I don't know why my father is so worked up about me meeting someone. I mean, I'm perfectly happy by myself.

My father sighs and leans over, and kisses my forehead. "Alli, you know I love you so much. I also know you have a heavy weight on your shoulders because of me. You don't need to worry about me. Please don't hold yourself back because of your mother's mistakes."

I can feel my eyes sting with tears. I swallow hard and rub my eyes before any tears can escape. I hug my dad again, and he doesn't pull away until I do. "I love you, dad. You don't know how much I needed to hear that. Thanks for inviting me out today. I missed this."

"Anytime, baby girl! I'm always here if you need me, even when you don't. I'm here."

I wave goodbye to my dad as I pull out of the parking lot. I feel like a weight has been lifted off of me, making me feel hopeful. When I get home, I immediately plop onto my couch and turn on the TV. My phone started buzzing, and I pressed answer without reading the caller ID. "Yes?" I sound so bored.

"Hey, girl! Guess where you and I are going tonight?"

I smile as soon as I hear Jessica's voice. "Um, well, I don't know about you, but I'll be in bed." I turn off the TV, knowing an argument is coming. 'No' is not in her vocabulary.

Jessica's voice raises an octave, and I must move the receiver away from my ear. "Oh no, you are not! I'm picking you up at nine for some dancing and drinks! You need to stop being a hermit and get yourself out there! I'm going to help you find yourself a real man. One that doesn't have orange fur."

"Hey! Don't bring Finn into this!" I defend my cat. She continues to argue and insists she is coming over. I groan and rub my forehead. "Jess… I want to stay home and binge-watch movies on Netflix." Sounds like my kind of night.

"Okay, one, that sounds so boring, and two, I am not taking no for an answer! Be ready by eight, or you are this… dead!" I hear the line click, and I groan.

"Hello?! Jessica!" I toss my phone onto the couch, feeling defeated and pissed. Just great! This wonderfully planned evening of sitting in my PJs and doing absolutely nothing is ruined. I enter my room and begin rummaging through my closet for something Jess-worthy to wear. I pulled out one of the only few dresses I owned. It's a short black number, and it's the one thing I have that is remotely 'sexy.' This is such a bad idea. Tonight, I am going to need more than one drink if I'm going to survive this fiasco.

I jump up when I hear a loud knocking on my front door. It can't be Jessica, I think to myself. It's too early. She rushes past me when I open the door and heads straight into my bedroom. Jessica was at my house before I could even prepare myself. I close the door and place my forehead against it. "Hey, Jess. Sure, you can come in," I mutter to myself. I am so not ready for this. Maybe if I stay here pressed against the door, she won't notice. She noticed.

Jessica comes to retrieve me, pulling me back to my room. She shoves me onto my bed and then narrows her brows, looking me up and down as if she's trying to solve the world's most challenging puzzle, "This is going to be a challenge."

I groan and let myself fall back onto the covers, "I think I'm just going to stay in. You go have fun without me." Jessica grabs onto my hands and drags me back up.

"Tonight, I am taking you out, and you're going to enjoy yourself for once! Come on. I need a friend tonight. Please." She gives me a dramatic pout, and I can't help but laugh.

"Okay, fine! You win. Hand me the black dress hanging up in the closet." There is no arguing with her, and I don't have the energy to try.

Chapter 7

Instead of handing me my dress, Jess pulls me until I'm standing and shoves me down in front of my vanity. She grabs the giant purse she brought with her and pulls a small cosmetic bag out of it, along with a straightener. She removes the small mirror from the vanity and sets it on the floor, making me nervous.

"You know, I can get myself ready, right?" I'm honestly terrified of what she will do to me. I imagine when she's through, staring into the mirror and seeing an over-exaggerated queen of the night looking back at me. She shushes me, ignoring my protests, and begins working. About halfway through, I try and peek at myself, and she scolds me.

"You can't see yourself until the end!" I pout and slouch in the seat, earning myself a pinch on the arm. I wince and sit up as straight as I can. She sticks her tongue out at me, and I roll my eyes. By the time Jessica finishes, my head is sore from all the pulling, and my eyelashes feel heavier than usual. I blink a couple of times, trying to get used to the feeling of the makeup on my face.

Jessica then throws me the short, black dress hanging in my closet. I slip it on quickly, feeling anxious to see myself. Jess walks me over to the full-length mirror, grinning. I brace myself for what I'm about to see, and my eyes grow wide when I do. The girl in the reflection looks beautiful! She looks like me, but a sexier and put-together grown-up version. My long hair is no longer wavy and frizzy but sleek and shiny. It looks like spun gold. I didn't realize how long my hair had gotten. I lean in closer and study my face. My light eyes sparkle against the subtle smoky eye, and I'm impressed by a winged liner. I smile because I look and feel beautiful. I even feel a little sexy for once. I turn to look at Jessica, smiling, and she nods approvingly.

"I am such a talented person." I grin wider at her and turn back to the mirror,

"WOW... -| don't know what to say, Jess! I feel really beautiful right now, thanks to you"

Jessica stands behind me and squeezes my shoulders softly. "Girl, you need more confidence! You don't see how beautiful you truly are. I did nothing but highlight your features, but you gave me a lot to work with."

I bite my lip and turn quickly, pulling her into a hug. Startled at my reaction, she makes a small noise of surprise but then wraps her arms around me. Jessica is the greatest friend I could've ever asked for. I honestly don't know what I would do without her in my life.

Jessica and I finish getting ready, and the sun has gone down by the time we are ready to go. When we arrive at Club Thirty-Eight, my short-lived confidence leaves me worried and regretful. I pick at my nails and self-consciously attempt to pull down the hem of my dress. I wish I had worn a dress that wasn't so short.

As soon as we enter the darkly lit club, Jessica heads for the bar, swinging her hips the entire way, exuding an aura like she owns the place. I wish had even a small ounce of her confidence. We sit down, and Jessica orders two drinks. We are sitting for no longer than five minutes when a very attractive man walks up and sits down beside Jessica. He flashes a sparkly white smile at her, and Jess lets out a giggle. He takes hold her one of her hands and brings it to his lips, kissing it softly. I choke on my drink and turn away quickly so that he can't see how hard I'm laughing.

"Hello. You are so lovely, and I couldn't help but notice your beauty from across the room. May I have the honor of buying you a drink?" Jessica smiles at him sweetly and then giggles again.

"Well, I already have one, but I wouldn't mind another!"

He chuckles, and I can't help but notice that he is still holding Jessica's hand, "My name is Richard, and you are?"

"It's Jessica, but you can call me Jess."

He glances over at me as if he's realizing that I was there and gives me the sweetest smile, "and what about your beautiful friend here?" My cheeks burn as I introduce myself. He nods attentively and then turns his full attention back to Jessica. I take another sip from my glass and turn away while they carry on their conversation. I feel a lump forming in my throat, and I can't help but wish I was back at home, safe under the covers.

Jessica and Richard are practically all over each other by the time their glasses are empty. Richard leans forward, his mouth brushing Jessica's ear, as he whispers something to her. She is biting her lips and looks like she's trying not to burst out laughing. I awkwardly sip the water I'd requested after finishing my first drink. I wasn't really in the mood to wake up the next morning with a hangover.

I cover my mouth as a yawn escapes. It was getting too late for me. Jessica hops out of her seat and says through hiccuped giggles, "Hey, Alli, I'm going to show this one some moves over on the dance floor. Do you mind?"

I do mind, but I shake my head and give her a small reassuring smile. Her eyes light up, and she pulls Richard away onto the dance floor. They waste no time and are grinding on each other like no one else is in the room.

On second thought, waking up with a hangover doesn't seem as bad an idea as sitting here alone and sober. I think it might have been after the third drink that I start feeling a little sick. I hop off of the stool I was sitting on and blindly make my way through the club.

Chapter 8

The lights and blaring music are too much for me right now, and I need fresh air. When I am finally outside, I let out a sigh of relief. The cold air feels nice compared to the stuffy air inside. I spot a bench and sit down, thankful for some peace and quiet. My head starts to pound, and I have to close my eyes, so I don't vomit. My eyes snap open when I feel a firm grip on my shoulder.

Expecting to see Jessica, I smile when I look up. It immediately fades when I see an older man, whom I've never seen before, grinning down at me. I shrug his hand off of my shoulder and stand up to head back inside. Why did I come out here alone when creepy people are lingering around? The man grabs a hold of my wrists and yanks me back. He is still grinning, and I try and pull my hand back, but he tightens his grip in response. A wave of terror courses throughout my body. He pulls me into him, and I almost gag as his breath hits my face. He reeks of alcohol and something else I can't quite pick out. My eyes well up with tears, and I try to pull away again, but his grip is too strong.

"Aww, come on now, pretty girl. Come on over to my place and play with me." One of his sweaty hands slides down onto the bare skin of my legs. My skin prickles with goosebumps, and I start to fear the worst. Please, let someone see us and help me. I try and let out a scream as his fingers start pulling up the hem of my dress, but all that comes out is a choked sob. The old man leans in and breathes heavily onto my neck. His lips press up against my flesh, and almost gag. I close my eyes tightly and try to block everything out. I pray that it will be over soon.

As if my prayers were heard, the man moves swiftly away from me. I immediately fall to my knees, unable to continue standing, as sobs shake my entire body. This night is turning into my worst nightmare.

"What the hell do you think you are doing, you sick bastard?" My head snaps up when I hear that voice. I have to blink away the tears to make him out. My mouth drops open in shock when I see who it is. It's that jerk I spilled my coffee on! An image of me flipping him off after our horrible run-in flashes in my head. The rage on his face terrifies me, and I'm afraid of what he is about to do. His anger when I spilled the coffee on his immaculate suit is nothing compared to this.

I watch in horror as he slams the older man into a wall. His fingers curl around the man's-stained shirt keeping him in place. "I am going to rip your throat out if ever see you lay a hand on her again. Next time I won't hesitate to end you." His knee comes up and slams into the old man's groin. He buckles over, groaning in pain but is yanked back up before he can crawl away. He cries out in a frightened voice and begins pleading for forgiveness. Ignoring the old man, he raises his fist into the air.

"NO! Please. Just stop! You could kill him!" I cry out. Afraid that if he hits him again, he won't be able to stop. I have gotten to my feet at this point, and I'm already by his side. I grab hold of his raised arm, hoping it'll keep him from striking. "Please, it's not worth it." My voice comes out as a shaky whisper, and I pray he's heard me.

His dark eyes flicker to mine, and my stomach flips. I can feel the tears spilling down my face. His expression softens, and his arm lowers. He turns back to the older man and immediately clenches his jaw. I'm afraid he's changed his mind when he throws the old man away forcefully. His face is stern, and his eyes are cold. He looks like he's trying to control his anger. I suddenly remember what happened when I spilled a cup of coffee on him at the coffee shop, and he flipped out. But now, all of a sudden, everything changes. He's looking at me with concern in his eyes, and his arm lowers as if he wants to reach out to me.

What's going on? Is he going to hit me? My voice comes out as a shaky whisper, "It was me," but I'm not sure if he heard me. He doesn't seem to recognize me. Maybe that's a good thing. We didn't exactly end on a good note.

His dark eyes flick back up to mine, then soften as recognition dawns on his face. "Hey," he says gently. "I don't know how you did it, but somehow… you've made me feel better than I ever have before," I say.

He seemed shocked when he saw me. I heard he had been waiting around the coffee shop looking for me after the last incident, but I never thought it would be like this. We didn't even say hello; we just looked at each other for a few seconds, and then he turned back to me once he realized it was me.

This man is a complete stranger that came to my rescue. I splashed a cup of coffee on him at the coffee shop and flipped him off. My opinion of him changed immediately because I was thinking, this is a kind man. He protects damsels in distress and beats the hell out of men who attempt to molest ladies. He didn't help because he knew me but because it was the right thing to do.

And then something happened that I never expected: He turned back around to face me and apologized for his behavior! He said he was sorry for making me feel uncomfortable, and then he told me that he realized it was me who had splashed the cup of coffee on him. He admitted he overreacted and probably deserved it. He was being rude to me! I'm shocked.

"I am sorry for splashing a cup of coffee on you," I said. "Thank you for your help in getting me out of that creep's grasp. I just wanted to take this opportunity to let you know how much your help means to me, especially when I'm having a bad day like this one. Your kindness is greatly appreciated."

"Anything for you, tiny warrior," he said with a chuckle.

"Huh?"

"Never mind. Let's get you home safely."

Chapter 9

The alarm clock blared loudly, the sound instantly waking me up from my slumber. I opened my eyes and got up. I scratched my head. Everything that happened last night is still etched in my mind. I didn't drink much alcohol yesterday, so I can remember everything vividly.

"Thank you for your help in getting me out of that creep's grasp. I just wanted to take this opportunity to let you know how much your help means to me, especially when I'm having a bad day."

His face formed a small smile.

"You don't need to thank me." He said. " I would have done it for any woman. Some creepy men like that guy don't know when to take a hint.

I chuckled. "He really was a creepy man."

"Right? I don't know what I would have done if you didn't stop me." He said it while chuckling.

"Well, nevertheless, I still want to thank you. I appreciate it."

"Anything for you, tiny warrior"

"Huh?"

Never mind. Let's get you home"

"I truly can't thank you enough."

He nodded his head. "Well, if you insist." he chuckled.

I planted my palm on my face. "I'm so silly." I didn't even catch your name.

"My name is Maximilian, but my friends call me Maxum." He said. He put out his hand for a shake.

"Nice to meet you, Maxum. My name is Alexandra, but you can call me Alli."

"Meow. Meow."

Finn snapped me out of my thoughts and back to reality.

"Meow meow." He purred at my legs. He looked hungry and weak. I crouched on my knees to rub him. Finn purred at me happily. He loved it when I rubbed him.

Whatever. I need to snap out of it. I need to feed Finn and get to work.

"My baby. You must be hungry. I'll get you some food."

I opened the mini-fridge. I grabbed Finn's food and placed it in his bowl. The red bowl has 'Finn' engraved on it. He happily devoured it all.

I shook my head at the sight. Finn sure loves to eat. I need to get ready for work.

****

I looked at the time on my wristwatch; I am running late again. I am fifteen minutes late. I hastened my pace. In no time, I reached the shop and walked in hastily.

I look around. Thankfully. There aren't any customers yet because it's early morning. Jessica is wiping down the counter.

Ian, the Manager, glared at me. He is in his late forties and doesn't get mad often, so I must have pissed him off.

"Alli, you are late." He said. His glaring made me feel on edge.

"Sorry, sir," I muttered.

"I notice you have been coming late for your shift," he said, rolling his eyes. "Care to explain yourself?"

I couldn't look him in the eyes. I clasped my hands nervously. I didn't think he would be so mad. This job was pretty easy and convenient because the commute was short, so I didn't want to mess up a good thing and get fired.

"Yeah, uhh, sorry," I said quietly. "It won't happen again, sir."

He sized me up and let out a breath. "I'm gonna be keeping my eyes on you. Just get to work.."

I nodded my head. "Thank you, Ian. Thank you!" He walked to the back.

I hurriedly ran to the table, where Jessica was cleaning.

She raised her head up, and her face formed a small smile. She placed the cleaning cloth down.

"Hey, girl," she said, waving at me.

"Hey," I said quietly.

She tapped my shoulder. "Hey, don't mind, Ian. I heard him telling you off. He has been cranky since I got here, so he is just pouring out his frustration on you. Don't let him get to you," she said.

"I don't know. He seemed really mad today." I scratched my neck nervously.

"You know how he is." She said, leaning on the table. "Focus on your work, and you should stop showing up late for work. Don't give him any reason to fire you."

I nodded my head. "Alright," I said. "Thanks for the pep talk." The talk with Jessica really helped me out. I need to focus and do my work so well that it will shut him up. I realize I have been taking the work for granted. I live so close to the coffee shop that it's unacceptable to drag in like this. I need to buckle down.

"You are welcome, girl." She said it with a small smile.

I let out a deep breath. "Okay, let me get started."

I rolled up my sleeves and cleaned the table next to Jessica's. After I cleaned that table, I moved on to the next one and then the next one. I don't know how much time passed, but do know I cleaned a lot of tables. I wiped the sweat from my brow as we finished up. I looked over, and Jessica was by the register. She was done with her prep for the first set of customers. Looking around, I noticed Ian was watching me. He seemed satisfied and less stressed. At least he can see I am working hard.

Four customers walked in simultaneously. One young adult couple and two female friends. They all looked like they were possibly in college. Most mornings, we never have more than four customers at a time, but in the afternoons and at night, the number of customers increases drastically, making weekends the worst days to wait tables. Or, the best when we get good tippers.

I walked quickly to one of the tables to take their orders. I grab my notepad from the register before heading to the customers. I started with ladies.

"Good morning. Welcome to Forever Cafe. What can I get you?"

"Well, can I get a decaf latte?" The friend with blonde hair said

"Okay." I wrote it down diligently with my notepad. "And what about you, miss?"

"I will have an espresso." The other female friend said. She is a brunette and never takes her eyes away from her phone.

I write it down on my notepad.

"Okay. Are you guys eating anything?"

They both nodded their heads simultaneously.

"Two slices of chocolate cake, please." The blonde girl said

"Okay. Coming right up." I said before, hurriedly walking away.

I walked to the kitchen and gave them the order. I had to move to the next table. I looked over, and Jessica was manning the register, so I still have to serve the next table. *Great. More work for me.*

I walked over to the next table. I put on a fake smile. The couple looked like they were in their late twenties.

"Good morning. Welcome to Forever Cafe. What can I get you?"

The group immediately looked at the menus.

"I would like an espresso." The guy said.

His lady's head is buried in the menu. She seemed undecided.

"Can I have a latte?" She asked,

"Alright, one espresso and a latte," I repeated. I scribbled it down in the notebook. "Anything else?"

"Can we also have a breakfast pizza?" The guy said.

I scribbled it down on the notepad. "Okay. Coming right up."

I took both menus from the table, and then I dashed over to the kitchen to give them to the chef.

"Here are the orders," I said, handing it to him. Chef Martin has been working here for a long time.

"Thanks, kid, coming right up." He said.

After several hours of work, my shift is finally over. I can finally go home. I'm so tired. I have been standing for hours. Jess and I are both in the staff room, changing and getting our bags.

"Let's go to this new Chinese restaurant that just opened," she said.

She changed into a crop top and left her dark jeans on. She looks so energetic. After a long day of work. She should be tired, but nope, she looks normal.

"I don't know; I just want to go home and nap."

"Boo," she said, rolling her eyes. "You are always at home. Don't you get bored?"

I shook my head. "Nope. Besides, Finn is waiting for me."

She let out a laugh. "Girl. You are too young to be an old cat lady," Jess teases.

I'm nowhere near a cat lady! How could she say that? I see Finn as my baby. I flipped her off. "I'm not an old cat lady."

That made her laugh harder. "I'm just saying."

"Whatever."

She tapped my shoulders. I folded my arms. "C'mon, please." She was pouting. "Pretty, please; come with me."

Chapter 10

The ambiance of the restaurant is amazing. "The Noodle Garden" is boldly emblazoned with neon lights. There are two waiters on standby. I honestly feel like I'm under-dressed for this place. There weren't a lot of customers. It is literally just us and two other sets of customers—a group of high school students at a table and a married couple with their two kids. Surprisingly, I am really hungry after a long shift.

We both sat down at a table. A waiter walked up to us. He handed us two menus.

"Hello. My name is Kai. Welcome to the Noodle Garden," he said. "What can I get you?"

I looked at the menu. There were so many good options.

"Can I have chicken and vegetable lo mien, please?" I said. My eyes were still fixated on the menu.

"I want chicken fried rice and fried chicken wings," Jessica said.

The waiter writes it down in his notebook. "Okay. What

about drinks?"

"Iced tea." We both said it simultaneously.

"Okay, coming right up." He said before walking away.

"This place is really nice," I said, glancing around.

"Yeah, you know I never miss it when it comes to food," she said, smirking.

I placed my arms on the table.

New customers walked in. To my utmost surprise, I recognized one of them immediately. It is Maxum and another guy. They walked side by side.

Oh no. I didn't think I would see him again after that night at the club. I know he saved me, and I owe him, but I'm still flustered to see him again. As he walked towards us, our eyes met. I quickly averted my gaze and used my palm to cover my face. Jessica shot me a funny look.

"What is wrong with you? You are acting weird," she said.

"Remember the guy that saved me at the club from that perv? He just walked in with a friend." I whispered.

Her eyes flew open. She turned her head to see. "No way. What are the odds?" She said, "That hot guy from the club?"

"Shhh, they are walking over here. Be quiet." I said this while putting my index finger up to my lips.

"Alexandra, right?" He said it while smirking.

"Yeah. You remember."

He nodded his head. "Yes, I do. What are the odds?"

"Forgive me. This is my best friend, Jessica. Jessica, meet Maximilian or Maxum." He sticks out his hand to shake hers. She reciprocated.

"Nice to meet you again." She said.

"Yeah, I remember. I also saw you at the club." He said. "By the way, this is my friend Simon. Simon, this is Alexandra and

Jessica."

"Hi." He spoke shyly. "Nice to meet you both."

Simon has dark hair. He is about the same height as Maximilian. They are both very tall and broad-shouldered. Simon extended his hand to shake both of ours. He shook mine first, then Jessica's.

"Nice to meet you, Simon," I replied.

"Well, Simon and I will get to our table," Maxum said.

Finally, They are going to their table.

"You guys can sit next to us. The table next to ours is empty." Jessica said.

Jessica, that sly fox. What is she up to? I shot her a look. She ignored me and kept smiling at them.

"No, we don't want to intrude. " They both said.

"Of course, you won't. You guys should sit down." She replied.

"Well, if you insist."

They sat at the table next to us. They were literally sitting next to us. From the outside, I'm sure it would appear as if we were coupled up.

The waiter walked to our table and placed the food and drinks.

Finally, I thought I would never eat.

"Thank you," Jessica said.

"Thanks," I say.

"Enjoy your meal." The waiter said

I clasped my hands together and dig into the food. Everything tasted amazing. In no time, we finished eating our meals.

The waiter walked over to Maximilian and Simon.

"Good afternoon, sirs. What will you both be having?"

"Two chicken fried rice and fried chicken wings," Maximilian said.

The waiter wrote it down on his notepad. "Coming right up." He walked away.

"So, how did you guys meet?" Maxum said. He pointed at us.

"We grew up in the same neighborhood and went to high school together," I replied. "Jessica has been my best friend for as long as I can remember. Even as years passed and I outgrew other friends. The two of us stuck together."

"That's cool," Maxum said. "Simon and I went to the same college."

"I'm sure you were a player," Jessica said, chuckling.

I let out a laugh. "Yeah, he looks like that type."

He shook his head. "Nope, I wasn't really a player."

"He is lying. This guy was a big player on campus. Girls were always flocking around him. I lost track of the number of girls he had. He was a real heartbreaker." Simon interjected.

Simon had been quiet since they sat. I'm surprised he is talking more; he is definitely coming out of his shell. I can already picture girls flocking around him. I mean, I can't blame them. He is a handsome guy, as much as I would hate to admit it.

Maxum shot Simon a look. "Dude." He said it quietly. His cheeks turned red.

This is a new side of him that I am seeing. He looks genuinely embarrassed.

"You see, I knew you were a player," I said, pointing at him.

"Well. Anyway, what can I say? College is like that, I guess. There is always a potential love interest lurking around." He said, folding his arms.

He really is a player. Even the way he walks. I pity his girlfriend. She has a lot to deal with.

"Yeah, you are right," Jessica said, chuckling. "About the love interests. In high school, that's how it was for me."

For as long as I have known Jessica. she has always had a long list of suitors. She is the kind of girl guys notice and approaches easily. She is very pretty and stands out in the room. She is never single for long. Even though she is single presently, I know it won't last long.

He nodded his head. "What about you, Miss Alli? Many love interests in high school?"

Everyone's attention turned toward me. All eyes were on me, and I hate being the center of attention. I shook my head. "Nope, not really. I was focusing on school back then." I had never been in a relationship. Apart from crushes and the elementary school kiss from spin the bottle and a kiss from truth or dare in high school. I had never had a proper boyfriend, not even in high school. I wasn't the type of girl guys would approach. I went through a tomboy phase, which didn't help my dating prospects, but I wasn't about to tell him all that. That is embarrassing.

"What about now?" he asked further.

"Nope, I'm focusing on work," I replied. "What about you?"

"Same. I'm just focusing on work."

"What about you, Jessica?" Simon asked.

"Nope. I'm single." She replied.

"Oh, really. Same here." He said it with a small smile. She smiled back at him.

I knew that look. I have seen it too many times. That is the look a guy gives Jessica when he is interested.

The waiter walked up with their food. He placed it on their table.

"Thank you." Maxum and Simon said simultaneously. "Can we get some water, please?" Simon asked.

The waiter nodded. "Certainly, coming right up."

They started eating, and Maxum seemed to be really enjoying the meal.

"You are such a foodie," I said. I was poking fun at him.

"Yeah, I am. I admit it." He said it while chuckling.

Running into Maxum wasn't as bad as I thought it would be. He is actually a cool guy. We enjoyed their company for a little longer and then made our exit.

Chapter 11

My doorbell rang incessantly. On my weekends off, I normally sleep away all the stress from the week. I normally spend my days in a hoodie and sweats, doing some Netflix and chilling under my covers. I got up from my bed, rubbing my eyes as I walked to the door. Who could it be at my door? Jessica knows better than to come on weekends. She normally goes out on a date or hangs out with other friends, and it's not like I have a boyfriend. I unlocked the door and swung it open to reveal my dad.

"Hey, Alli cat," Dad said, kissing my cheek.

Of course, it is my dad. Who else it would have been? Dad drops by sometimes to check on me but not often because he is busy with work too. He works as a site manager for a construction company and has been working there most of my life. "Dad!" I exclaimed excitedly. He pulled his arms out for a hug, and I reciprocated and hugged him back.

"Can I come in now?" he said, chuckling.

"Of course. " I said.

He walked in, and I shut the door behind him. He sat down on the couch, and I plopped next to him. He examined me and chuckled. "I can't believe this is how you are spending your weekend."

I folded my arms. "Dad, you know I love staying home."

He looked bewildered. "When I was your age. You couldn't catch me home on a weekend."

"Yeah, I know, but we are different."

"You should be more like me. It's either I had a hot date, or my friends and I spent the weekend partying."

Picturing my Dad at my age raging like tomorrow is a funny sight. It isn't hard to believe. He always told me how his college years were the best years of his life. "Wow, so you were a party animal," I said, tapping his shoulder.

His eyes lit up, remembering the past. "Yes, you know; I was one of the most popular guys on campus. I wonder how my liver survived all that. I partied nonstop. I honestly can't lie. College was a blast."

"If College was really about partying. I'm glad I didn't go," I said, flashing a grin he didn't reciprocate. It was meant to be a joke, but it seemed he didn't find it funny.

He let out a deep breath. "Sometimes I forget you didn't go. Then you remind me." Dad never got over the fact that I didn't go to college. Of course, he respects my decision and never tried to force his opinion on me, but he was still sad from time to time. I didn't want to go to college simply because I didn't want to be in student debt, and I didn't wanna put my dad through that. I knew he couldn't afford it. It took him twenty years to pay his student loans, and he is now finally relieved.

It's not like I am passionate about anything. My dad suggested community college, but I didn't feel the need to go through college at all, and I had average grades back in high school, so a scholarship was not an option. I still feel a college degree isn't necessary. Just because it's the conventional thing to do, that doesn't mean everyone has to go that route. I shook my head. "Yeah, sorry about that but like I always say, not everyone needs College."

He glanced at me. "I'm sure one day. You will come around." Dad actually thinks one day I'll change my mind and magically go to college. Like it's that easy.

I adjusted my seating position. "Highly unlikely." I retorted.

"Never say never, baby girl."

I was going to agree with him because I didn't want to argue with him today. He hasn't visited in a while, so I want peace. I nodded my head. "Alright. Got it. Do you want anything to eat? I can order a pizza," I said, tapping my phone.

He shook his head. "Nope, I'm not feeling hungry. I actually came to talk to you." He said. He sounded nervous, and his demeanor changed. I wonder what this is all about. He let out a deep breath. "Alli, I have been wanting to tell you this for a while now." He scratched his neck nervously.

"What is it, dad? You know you can tell me anything." I grab his arm.

"Well, I'm seeing someone."

My eyes flew open. "Really?" After he and Debbie decided they were better off as friends, I thought that was the end. It took him forever to work up the nerve to ask her out. I thought for sure he wouldn't try again. As long as I can remember, Dad didn't really date. He focused most of his energy on raising me. He dated sporadically over the years but nothing serious.

"Yeah. Well, say something." He said. For him to tell me about his girlfriend, he must really like her. I actually want my dad to find someone he can spend the rest of his life with. I always pestered him to date, but he mostly shrugged it off.

"Dad." I began. "I'm really happy for you, really."

His face formed a smile. "I'm glad." He seemed relieved by my response. As much as I love my dad, I wasn't going to put a damper on his happiness. I know my opinion meant a lot to him.

I tapped him playfully, "So tell me about the lucky lady."

."Well, her name is Megan, and we met in a book club I joined recently. She is three years younger than me, and she has two daughters. We have been dating for a month, and she is really nice. You would like her."

Hearing my dad speak about a woman makes me happy. It's really heartwarming. I can tell from the look on his face that he is smitten. "Well, it's about time you got a girlfriend! I have been telling you for years."

His cheeks turned red. "Alli, stop it!" He muttered.

"OMG, you are totally blushing." I burst into laughter.

He used his palm to cover his cheeks. "No, I'm not." He is acting like a teenager, blushing and everything. It's just nice to tease him.

"You so are," I said, chuckling,

He rolled his eyes. "What are you laughing about? Young lady." He stood up from the couch. "I think I'm just going to go." He started walking away.

"No, don't go," I said, grabbing his arm as he moved. "Stay. I'm not laughing anymore."

He stopped in his tracks and sat back down. "Okay, but no more laughing at your old man."

I nodded. "Okay, no more laughing," I said with a smile. I sat back down on my couch.

"But seriously, I would love you to meet Megan eventually. Would you be cool with that?" He said, crossing his legs.

"Of course, Dad. I'm happy to meet her whenever you want."

He ruffled my hair. "That's my girl."

My phone rang. The sound blared loudly. It's Ian, the manager of the coffee shop. "One second," I said. Dad keeps quiet and folded his arms as I accepted the call.

"Hello."

"Alli, I'm sorry to disturb you on a weekend, but I'm gonna need a huge favor."

"What is it?"

"Can you cover Rory's shift this evening?"

"What, why? You know I don't like weekend shifts."

"I know, but her daughter is sick, so she can't make it today. She has to stay home and take care of her."

I suddenly felt bad. I just assumed he was trying to overwork me. "Oh well. That can't be helped."

"So, will you help?"

I let out a deep breath. "Fine. I'll do it."

"Thank you. Thank you."

"You are paying me overtime."

"Deal."

Chapter 12

Spending my Saturday in the coffee shop wasn't on my shortlist. The shop is packed with customers, and guess who has to serve them? I just got here, and I already miss my bed.

"C'mon, stop frowning," Ian whispered. "Perk up a little. It isn't that bad."

"Sorry, Boss, I can't fake it."

Ian chuckled. "Hey, you have to fake it till you make it."

My face formed the fakest smile ever. "Happy now? "

Ian chuckled. "At least it's better. Now I don't feel so bad. You are not the only one here on a weekend shift. I'm here."

"Yeah, that makes me feel soooo much better," I muttered with an eye roll.

"What?"

"Nothing." Bussing tables is exhausting. Standing for hours on end is no fun. I walked to a table with a family of four. A couple with twin girls who seems to be about two years old. The couple looked like they were in their mid-twenties. "Good evening. My name is Alli. Welcome to Forever Cafe. What can I get you?"

"Two espressos and three slices of cheesecake, please," mom said.

I wrote it down in my notepad and nodded my head. "Alright, coming right up." One of the baby girls was drooling, and it ran down her face. The other baby girl is clapping her hands playfully. They are both so adorable. "Oh, your baby is drooling. Let me get a napkin for her."

The mother's attention flew to her daughter. She looked amused. "Okay, thank you."

I run over to the counter and grab a hand full. I walk to the back to give Chef the order. Running back to the table, I hand over the napkins.

"Thank you." She said.

"You are welcome," I said with a small smile. I rub the baby's cheek with my thumb. "Your babies are beautiful. What are their names?" I always go gaga for babies.

She holds both of their hands with a smile. "Thank you. This is Bella and Priscilla."

I hold their tiny hands. "Cuties." I walk back to the register. A new customer walks in. I raise my head up, and it is Maxum and a woman. They are walking side by side. She looked like a model with her slender frame and long legs. She has blonde hair. Maxum is such a player. I thought he was focusing on work, and here he is out on a hot date. There are so many fancy restaurants. I don't know why he would choose this cafe. My cafe!

"Alli. Go wait on the next customers." Ian said.

I definitely don't want to serve Maxum and his date, but there is nothing I can do. There are no other waitresses. It's literally just me. I glance at the table, and Maxum and his date are happily chatting away. They look engrossed in their conversation. I let out a breath. "Okay." I walk as slowly as humanly possible to their table, dragging my feet. "Good evening. Welcome to Forever Cafe. What can I get you?"

"Hey, Alli," Maxum said with a wave.

"You know her?" The date said. She looked surprised.

He nodded his head. "Yeah, she's a friend." He said. "Alli met Tania. Tania meets Alli."

Tania reached out her hand for a shake. "Nice to meet you."

"Nice to meet you too," I said, reciprocating the handshake. Maxum leaned his arm on the table. Tania was texting on her phone. "So what can I get you guys?"

Maxum and his date both looked through their menu. She glanced fervently at the menu. "I don't know what to choose. Everything looks so good."

He tapped her arm and asked, "Should I order for both of us?"

Her face formed a small smile, and she nodded, "Yeah, you can do that. I don't mind."

"Two espressos and two scones," he said, glancing at the menu. "Is that okay with you?"

"Of course, it's okay. I don't mind anything."

I wrote everything down in the notepad and nodded my head, "Okay, coming right up." I walked back and gave the Chef the order. I leaned against the counter and waited for their food. After a while, Chef rang the bell, and I walked quickly to table number five. The couple with twins. I carried the tray with my hand and placed it on the table.

"Thank you," The mom said.

"You're welcome. Enjoy your meal."

Maxum kept stealing glances at me. I'm sure he thinks I don't notice, but I notice almost immediately. He is on a date, yet he keeps looking at me. He really is a player. Asshole. The bell rang. I ran to the back, picked up the food and drinks on a tray, and walked to table seven. To Maxum and his date. I walked over steadily.

"Okay, Two espressos and two scones." I place their food on their table.

"Thank you," Tania said. "This looks good."

"Thank you," Maxum said. His eyes were still fixated on me.

After a few hours, my shift ended, and I was clocking out. The cafe was significantly empty except for two customers. Maxum and Tania are about to leave. They both got up and walked out. Maxum hailed a cab for her. He hugged her, and she reciprocated the hug. "Let's do this again some other time." He said, waving her off.

"It was nice catching up." She said. She got into the cab, and it rolled away.

I shook my head and walked to the bus stop. It's only a couple of blocks, but I'm beat. A car horn blared loudly. I looked up from my phone.

"Hey," Maxum said. He stopped his car and is in the middle of the road.

"Hey."

"Let me drop you off." He said earnestly

I didn't wanna bother him. He just had a date, so I didn't want any misunderstandings. I shook my head. "No need. Just go ahead."

"C'mon, I don't bite. What do you say?" He said with a smile.

Well, a free ride is a free ride. I let out a deep breath. "Okay fine." I walked to the car and hopped in. I put on my seat belt, and he sped off. There was silence for a while. Frankly, I didn't know what to say. The ride was awkward.

"Why are you so quiet? Are you worried I'm an ax murderer?" He said, chuckling.

I folded my arms. "Please. I don't think an ax murderer would take an espresso with extra whipped cream,"

He turned on the radio and The Weekends' raspy voice blared through the speakers. He let out a laugh. "Aha, There's my tiny warrior."

"Hope your girlfriend is cool with you dropping me off. I don't wanna cause any misunderstanding."

His eyes flew open. "She is not my girlfriend. Tania and I are just friends. I haven't seen her in a while, so we were catching up."

I didn't even ask him, and I made my own conclusions. I have to work on that. "Well, it seemed more than catching up. From what I could see." I said, folding my arms.

He chuckled. "So you were spying on us.." He replied. He hitches his brow.

"You were at my workplace. I wouldn't call that spying."

"That's true. Anyway, it wasn't a date. We were just chilling. Everything was very casual."

Why did I have the feeling she thought it was a date even if he didn't? "Well, She seemed interested in you."

He shook his head, "I doubt that; we have been friends for years. I'm sure she would have told me if she had any interest."

"Maybe I read the situation wrong."

"Yeah, you did," he said. He glanced at me.

"Well, if you do want to go on a date. A real one. Don't come to my workplace. It's gross."

He let out a laugh, "Trust me when I'm going on a real date. It's gonna be a fancy restaurant with a girl I actually like."

I rested my back. "Good luck with that."

He turned and looked at me. His face formed a small smile.

No wonder he always got the girls, he is a handsome guy, and being this up close and personal, I see how easy it is to get lost in those eyes. In no time, he parked in front of my apartment. He turned off the ignition.

"Thanks for the ride," I said.

He scratched his neck nervously, "So, can I get your number?"

Chapter 13

The sheer rush you feel when someone is giving you attention is exhilarating. I felt like a teenager when my phone lit up with messages from him. As someone with a lack of male paramours, this is exciting. This is the most action I have gotten in a while. Maxum and I have been texting for days. I didn't know how to read him. Sometimes he's flirtatious and other times he'd feel more like a friend. I had never had a boyfriend, so I didn't know if maybe I am misreading the signs. We texted for hours on end. We never seemed to run out of things to talk about. But he makes everything so casual I doubt he is actually interested in me. If he is, he would say something.

The Alarm clock blared loudly, jolting me up from my sleep. I had to get to the gym. I'm always late, but I'm trying to make an effort; plus, Jessica will kill me. She got the gym memberships for us. Apparently, it's unhealthy to spend all your free time eating bags of potato chips and watching South Park; at least, that's what Jessica says. I think she is just a hater. I stretched and yawned. Darn it. I can't believe it is morning already. I wanted to sleep a little longer, but I have to get up and get going. I pull out a gray sports bra with matching leggings to change into. My ringtone blared loudly. *Speaking of the devil.*

My caller ID displayed Maxum. He didn't call often. He preferred texting, so I am surprised he's calling. I answered and placed the call on speaker so that I can finish dressing. "Morning," I said, coughing awkwardly.

"Yeah, Morning. You sound chipper. I wasn't sure if you would be up yet."

"Yeah, I'm heading to the gym soon. Why are you up already?" I removed my pajamas, get dressed, and pull my hair in a ponytail.

"I am home but working."

"Oh, and you couldn't do that later in the day?"

"No. I have to do it now, or I will never get it done. I'm becoming a procrastinator."

Finn appeared from under my bed, surprising me. He purred on my legs. "Meow." I placed my index finger on my lips and shushed him. He always comes at the wrong time. He's probably hungry.

"Is that a cat I am hearing?"

"Uh..yeah"

"I didn't take you for a cat, lady," he said, chuckling.

"Shut up."

That prompted further laughter from his end.

"You seem to be enjoying yourself."

"Don't mind me. What is the name of your cat?"

"His name is Finn."

"It's funny I didn't see you as a pet person."

"Why?"

"I don't know. You didn't seem like you'd like pets. Let alone have a cat."

"Well, I love Finn. He's my baby"

"I'm going to leave you so you can get going."

"Okay, no problem…we will talk later." I hung up the call. My phone pinged.

Maxum sent a photo. I download the picture. It is a selfie of him smiling at his desk with his laptop with a text that reads "Later Loser"

I stared at the picture. Damn. He is lucky he is so hot

****

I love exercising. It's another way to relieve tension and keep my body fit. The gym I attend is very brutal, and there is no time to slack off. "Exercising isn't easy," I said, panting. Sweat dripped down my face. Jessica is right next to me, and she was also sweating and breathless. She is the one who pushed me to start exercising. I ran on the treadmill. My sports bra wiggled with my movements. I'm actually obsessed with gym clothes, though. They are so comfortable. I stocked up when we got the gym membership. I have been coming for a month now, and although it's stressful, I'm happy Jessica convinced me to join. We had been exercising for a while, so a break is needed.

"C'mon, now you are just being dramatic." She said, panting. She was on another treadmill beside me. She got down from her machine and drank water from her bottle.

"Can I have a sip?"

She handed the bottle to me. "Here you go, lazy bones."

I didn't realize how thirsty I was until I started drinking. I drank the remainder and handed back the empty bottle. Her eyes flew open.

"You finished all the water," she said. She laughed.

"My bad. I was just so thirsty," I said.

"No problem, ma'am. I'm here to serve you," she said, chuckling.

I smacked her hands playfully.

"Girl, I just remembered I have tea for you." She said, wiggling her body excitedly.

I love a good gab session. "Alright, girl. Spill the tea."

" Simon and I have been talking."

My eyes flew open. "Really?" I'm actually surprised. I know Jessica is really popular with guys, but they weren't giving off flirty vibes the day they met.

She flipped her hair. It was clear she was excited. Jessica easily falls for a guy. Her heart is really open. The smitten look she has on her face is one I have seen many times. "Yeah."

"Wow. Since when?" I asked.

"We exchanged numbers that day we met, and we have been talking for a while."

"You have been holding out on me," I said, crossing my arms.

"My bad. It's early days, you know?"

"Tell me everything. Are you guys exclusive?"

She shook her head. "No, not yet. But I'm sure he will ask me soon to be his girlfriend."

"Ohh. "

She coughed awkwardly. "Yeah…but it's not a big deal. We don't need to rush things." This coming from the girl who has already planned her dream wedding down to the entrees. I hope she's not settling. Jessica doesn't know how to discern a red flag in a relationship from a green flag. I was so engrossed in my thoughts I didn't hear her calling me.

"Alli?"

"Uh, what?" I responded. I was still dazed.

" I said I am just having fun ."

"So, are you guys hooking up?"

"No, Alli, we are not hooking up." She declared, flushing beet red. "We are just talking and seeing where things go."

"Oh, right. That's cool."

She tapped my arm playfully. "So what about Maxum?"

I had already filled Jessica in on Maxum. I told her immediately after we started talking. "We actually spoke this morning," I said, flipping my hair.

"Uhh, What did he say?" she exclaimed excitedly.

"We just talked for a bit. He found out about Finn."

Jess let out a laugh. "So he knows you are a cat lady now," she said, pointing at her.

"Well, I'm not a cat lady, but he knows about Finn."

"Honestly, I'm just happy you're finally getting some action. You really need to get laid."

"Shh, keep your voice down," I whispered with reddened cheeks. I looked around. People around us were not paying attention, thankfully.

She raised her hand up. "Okay fine, I'll be quiet."

"My problem with him is I'm not sure he likes me. I think he is just being friendly." I blurted shyly. My insecurity creeps out unexpectedly.

"I think he likes you. If not, he wouldn't be so consistent." Jessica, ever the optimist, was always confident about love.

"Right."

Her ringtone blared. "It's him," She whispered. She looked at me expectantly.

"What are you looking at me for? Just answer it."

She answered the call. It is a video call. "Hi" She waved at him. Simon appeared on camera. He looked like he was in bed. He waved back.

"Hey," he said, smiling sheepishly. "I can see you are at the gym."

"Yeah. I love working out. "

Why did I feel like I am a third wheel even though he isn't here?

"That's cool. I was too lazy to go today, but I'll go tomorrow before work."

"Oh, you are a slacker, I see," she said, chuckling. "Say Hi to Alli." She angled the phone to my side.

"Hey," I said, waving at him.

"What's up, Alli? How've you been?"

"I'm good," I say as I put on the fake smile. Jessica angled the phone back to herself.

"There is a pool party happening today, and I would love for you to come."

"Really?" She said with a small smile.

"Yeah. Alli, you should come too." He said.

I'm not really a fan of parties. I'm an introvert. I always choose my bed over a party or a club or generally socializing with people. I give in to Jessica's whims at times, though.

" Uh..okay," I said, folding my arms. "We will see."

"I'm not gonna hold you guys up. See you at the party."

I have absolutely no intention of going to the party.

Chapter 14

The party is filled with so many people; we came late as usual, so people are already in the pool. The pool is packed with people, while some were on recliners. Music was blasting through the speakers. People were conversing with their friends. Couples are dancing together while some couples were kissing and others were drinking. Some people were already drunk. People were using ping pong and pool tables. Others are playing drinking games. I folded my arms as I glare at Jessica. I really don't want to be here. "I can't believe you convinced me to come," I said.

Jessica held my hand. "Thank you, babe, for coming with me. I know this isn't your scene."

"Yeah. Yeah." I said, nodding. We walked further in.

Simon walked up to us. Maxum was right behind him. "I'm glad you guys made it," he said as waved hello. He pulled Jessica in for a hug. She reciprocated.

And now I can see the chemistry between the two of them.

"Hey, you," Simon said.

"Hey, Simon," Jessica replied. They released each other from the hug.

"Hey guys," Maxum said. His lips formed a smile, and he waved.

"Hey," I replied.

"Hey, Maxum," Jessica said.

He waved at her. "Hello."

"Let me get you guys some drinks,' Simon said.

"Yes, I love shots," Jessica exclaimed.

"I think ill just have one drink," I said. "I'm not much of a drinker."

He disappeared for a while and came back with shots.

I'm a lightweight, so I rarely drink alcohol, but since I'm at a party, I wanna get buzzed.

"Okay, everyone, let's party!" Simon said.

Everyone clinked glasses and took a shot.

Immediately after I tasted it, I can feel it kicking in. That's when I realized; I'm in trouble. Drinking ensued. One drink turned into two, then three. Then I lost track of how many shots I had. A few hours later, I started feeling quite dizzy. I'm seeing double. "I'm…uhh..I'm having so much fun." I slurred. I have a shot in my hand. Everything looked hazy. The party is hazier now. A lot of people were drunk. Others were grinding against each other. Jessica and Simon seemed to have disappeared a while ago. I tried walking, but I was stumbling.

"Easy now," Maxum said, chuckling. "You are so drunk." He held my hand to balance me. He held a drink in his hand but didn't appear drunk.

I shook my head. "No, I'm not. I'm fine."

He held his fingers out in front of me. "Oh really? How many fingers am I holding up?"

I squinted. I am definitely seeing double. "Ten," I said, chuckling. "Did I get it?"

"OK, warrior, you are definitely drunk," He said, smiling. "You are such a lightweight. I drank too, but I'm alright."

"That's because I'm a man and you are a woman, or am I a woman and you are the man?"

He looked around and rolled up his sleeves."I guess I have to step up and take care of you."

"Yeah, I'm a damsel in distress, and I need you to help." And that was the last thing I remembered before I became engulfed in darkness.

****

My eyes fly open. I have a splitting headache. My head throbbed. I'm feeling the hangover. I look around. Everything feels so strange, the bed, the room, everything feels off. This is definitely not my apartment. I glance down. I'm wearing a pajama top that is definitely not mine. Memories flashed in my head. I remember drinking shots. Stumbling while attempting to walk, and Maxum helping me. I can't remember anything after that. I glance around, and Maxum is at his computer typing away. My heart dropped. Fuck. What am I doing in his bed? I feel like the ground is about to swallow me. Why did I have to drink so much? Then it clicked. Oh no. Oh no. Did Maxum and I sleep together? "Ahh!!"

Maxum turned around and ran towards me. He grasped my shoulders with a concerned expression. "Are you alright?"

When he touched me, I immediately felt heat creep up my body. I moved a bit, pushing his hand off. "Maxum," I let out a deep breath. "Did anything happen between the two of us?"

He chuckled. "No, warrior, nothing happened. Get your

mind out of the gutter."

Relief filled my body. I breathed a sigh of relief.

"Wow, I have never seen a girl so relieved we didn't hook up. It's normally the other way around." He said, chuckling. "You're hell for my ego."

I am just glad nothing happened between us. That would make things awkward, especially since we are just friends. It would just complicate things, and I would hate to ruin our friendship because of a drunken mistake. "It's not funny."

"Yes, it is." He smirked. He sat next to me on the bed.

"So, how did I end up here?"

"Yesterday, you were so shitfaced." He said. "It was so funny. Jessica and Simon had slipped out, and I couldn't just leave you there. I'd never leave you defenseless."

That explains a lot. "What about my clothes?" I said, glancing at the pajamas.

"You threw up on yourself," He said, squinting at me. "It was so gross."

I felt so embarrassed. I covered my face with my palm. "Wow. I'm so sorry about that. Thanks for taking care of me."

He folded his arms. "It was my pleasure."

A realization dawned on me. For him to change my clothes. He had to see me in my underwear. My cheeks flushed in embarrassment. "Wait. So when you changed my clothes. You saw me in my underwear."

He nodded. "Yeah. Is there any other way to change someone's clothes without seeing their underwear? Unless they're not wearing any," he chuckled.

"Oh, okay. Just processing that information." Heat crept into my face. I can't believe he saw me in my underwear.

He slanted a look at me. "Hey. It's not a big deal. It's just like seeing you in a bikini." He said in a reassuring tone.

"I guess," I said, folding my arms.

He stood up from the bed suddenly and started unbuckling his belt.

"What are you doing?" I was taken aback. This sounds like the beginning of a bad porno.

"I'm stripping down to my underwear so that we will be even."

I covered my eyes with my palm. "No. That's okay."

He let out a laugh. "Open your eyes. I'm just messing with you."

I uncovered my eyes, and he was standing there smirking. He reached his hand out to me.

"C'mon, let me make you some breakfast." He said. "I'm sure you are hungry."

"Yeah, I could eat."

Chapter 15

Maxum is an incredible cook. I watched in awe as he made breakfast. It was ready in no time. He fried bacon, made toast, omelets, and brewed freshly ground coffee. He placed it on the coffee table; right in front of me.

"Thank you." When I tasted the food, I couldn't hold back a moan. Everything is so delicious. I'm a horrible cook. Me and dad lived off pizzas and sandwiches when he didn't have time to cook. The only thing I don't mess up is sandwiches- and that's because I make there's no way to mess them up. "This is so good." I said in between bites." I didn't know you could cook."

He sat next to me on the couch with his plate and switched on the Television. He flips to an episode of Morty and Rick! He lifted his fork and started eating. "I'm pretty sure I can cook better than you." He scoffed.

"I'm not arguing with you. If I attempted to cook, we would probably end up calling the fire department," I said in between bites. The breakfast is so delicious. I don't want to stop eating though I'm full.

He let out a laugh. "I would pay to see that happen. You are that bad at cooking?"

I nodded. "Worse."

"Okay."

"How did you learn to cook anyway?"

"My mom taught me, actually. She taught me all her recipes so they could be passed down because my sister Linda is horrible at cooking."

There is more to Maxum than meets the eye. He has so many layers that I didn't realize before. There are so many things I didn't know about him, and it's fun getting to know him little by little. "I guess there are a lot of things about you I didn't know. Huh?"

The Doorbell rang.

"Hold that thought," he said before walking to the door.

I'm already done with my breakfast, and I'm just drinking coffee at this point.

The Door opens, and in walks a woman in her early fifties. She has dark brown hair and sharp blue eyes. She looks rich. You can tell from her aura. She's wearing a pastel dress with matching heels that probably cost enough to pay my rent for a year. She is holding a large plate covered with foil. "Hello, son," she said. She walked in like she owned the place.

"Mom? What are you doing here?"I hear him shriek.

Wait, his Mom? This is awkward. Oh, My Gosh. What will she say when she sees a girl has slept over? The situation looks so bad. I get up and stand awkwardly.

"That's no way to greet your mother, Maximilian." She slants a look at him.

"Sorry, hi, Mom." He muttered. He looked uncomfortable. At least I'm not the only one finding everything uncomfortable.

Our eyes met each other. I felt like I was being analyzed. I had to say something. It's rude to stare. "Good morning," I said lamely.

Maxum stepped beside me. "Mom, this is Alexandra Hart. Alli, this is my Mom, Janette."

"Nice to meet you. Mrs. Greyson." I said shyly.

"Oh honey, just call me Janette." She replied.

"Alright, Janette," I said, nodding my head.

His mom nodded. She seemed to be good at hiding her emotions. I couldn't read her. I drank more coffee to calm myself.

"Maxum. Honey. Wow, you didn't tell me you found yourself a girlfriend. And a lovely one at that. She's gorgeous!" She said with a smile.

I coughed heavily. The coffee went down the wrong pipe. "I am not his girlfriend," I said while tapping my chest.

"Mom. We are not dating." He replied.

She looked confused. "Well, if you are not dating, are you guys doing what kids do these days? Is it frenemies or friends with benefits, you kids call it?"

"Mom!!" He shrieked, his cheeks flushed and stained beet red.

"What? I'm cool. No need to act coy with me, son," She said playfully.

"We are actually just friends," I muttered.

"Yeah, Mom, I just let her crash here for the night." He said.

She didn't look convinced. "If you say so. I'm just going to let it go." She winked at us.

I feel so awkward. She thinks we're hooking up.

"Mom!" he shrieked.

"What?" she said chuckling. She put her arms in the air. "Fine, I'll stop teasing."

"What did you bring with you?" He said pointing at it.

She tapped her head. "Oh yeah, I made you a casserole." She placed it on the countertop and then sat down with Maxum and me. She dropped her handbag on the table.

"So, Alli. Is it alright if I call that?" She slanted me a look.

"Yes, of course."

"Thank you, dear. Where did you meet Maximilian?"

Maxum looked rather uncomfortable, but he was trying to hide it. He scratched his neck nervously.

"Well. We met at a coffee shop." I replied.

"Oh, really, that's nice. And you guys clicked right away?"

It definitely wasn't a meet-cute. I'll say that. "Not really…we hated each other at first," I said, glancing at Maxum.

"We both got into an argument." He interjected. "There was a misunderstanding."

"What do you mean by misunderstanding?" Janette said. Her eye lit up in curiosity.

"Long story short. I accidentally spilled coffee on him." *This wasn't a story I ever thought I was gonna tell.*

She let out a laugh. . "Maxum honey, that must have stung."

"It did." He said, chuckling.

The Atmosphere was better now. The awkward energy seemed to have dissipated. I can finally relax.

"So, Alli," she said. "What do you do for a living?"

I'm sure she would love to hear I have a high-paying job. I know waitressing isn't the most glamorous job but it is what it is. I'm not ashamed of myself because it's honest work and I take pride in that. I'm independent and take care of myself.

"Mom. Stop badgering her!" Maxum protested.

"What? I'm just asking." She said, pouting.

"You are making her feel uncomfortable," he said. "No more questions."

"Fine," she said, raising her hands up in defeat. "No more questions."

"Thank you." He said with a deep breath. "Yeah. Mom, don't you have somewhere to be right now?" He slanted her a look.

She looked at him with a knowing smile. "Yeah, I actually have somewhere I need to be."

At least she can take a hint.

"Alright." He said.

"It was nice meeting you, Janette," I said, waving her off.

"Mom I'll walk you to your car," Maxum said, as he walked behind her.

She shook her head. "No need. You have a guest."

"Well if you insist." He said cutting her off.

"I'll see you some other time, Alli dear." She said waving at me. "Next time we meet, I'll show you some of his baby pictures."

"That I would love to see," I replied.

Janette seems like a nice lady, and I can definitely see myself Interacting with her in the future.

Maxum shook his head. "No, she won't," he whispered.

"Yes, she will," I whispered back to him.

"Bye, Mom."

"Bye, son." She said waving him off. And with that, she walked away, turning the door knob open before disappearing out of sight.

Maxum coughed awkwardly. "Sorry about my Mom, she stops by unexpectedly like that sometimes."

"That's no biggie. My dad literally just did that a few days ago."

He chuckled. "Parents. We are adults, but they still treat us as kids."

"Right?" I agreed, adjusting my seating position.

He stood up and took our dirty plates to the sink. I followed after him.

"Let me do that. It's the least I could do since you cooked"

"No, it's fine. It's literally just two plates and a frying pan" he said.

"Well, let me keep you company."

"I'll take it." He put the plates in the dishwasher and hand-washed the pan.

"See, I told you I don't need any help."

"Yeah, you are right."

He walked back to the couch to sit down, and I am right behind him. I wonder how his mother would react if I'd said I'm a waitress. I know we are just friends, but rich people look down on average people, so I'm not naive.

"Is everything okay? You seem out of it."

"Oh, it's nothing."

He wasn't convinced. He ruffled his hair. "It's definitely something. C'mon, spit it out."

"How would your Mom react if she found out I'm a waitress? Would she want us to stop hanging out?"

He smiles. "My mom doesn't care about all that. Yeah, it might seem like we have money, but my parents are self-made and started from nothing. They built their business from the ground up, so my mom knows what it is to struggle. She wouldn't flinch if you told her you are a waitress."

Hearing him talking about his family is really heartwarming. It really gives more insight into him. "What business are your parents in?"

"My Dad is the CEO of Greyson Inc, and my mom is one of the board members. I work there as well."

I have heard of their company before. They are very successful in their field. Greyson Inc is a Hedge Fund. It's a real family affair for everyone to work there. "Wow, that's so cool," I said. "No wonder you were so uptight when I spilled coffee on your suit the day we met. I almost ruined it." I chuckled.

"I was in a bad mood that day." He scoffed. "Anyway, let's forget about that."

"It's already forgotten." I said."Your Mom is really cool, though." I said, crossing my legs.

"Yeah, she is." He said with a small smile. "You did well today." He glanced at me with his piercing blue eyes, and my heart thumped. I don't know if it's just hormones or what, but this feeling in my chest is dangerous.

******

After an eventful time at Maxum's, I'm finally home. Home sweet home. His place is much nicer than mine but there is no place like home. It felt like I had been at his house for a week.

My phone pinged.

Hey. I heard from Simon that Maxum took your home. Hope you are good. I'm still hungover - Jessica.

I mentally remind myself to call Jess and yell at her. She just disappeared. I walked into my room and sat down on the bed. It's good to be back on my own bed. "Finn. Come here, boy." He normally greets me as soon as I open the door, and he should definitely be hungry, so I want to feed him. Finn didn't appear as usual. That's weird. I checked under my bed. His favorite hiding place. No luck. I check under the couch in the living room, and in the kitchen cabinets. Alarm bells started ringing in my head. Finn is missing.

"Finn!!" I yell, hoping he will hear me. I turn my whole apartment upside, frantically searching for him. This isn't like him to go missing. He is a very laid-back, peaceful cat. Even if he does go outside, he doesn't stay long. Panic is setting in. Where could he be? Finn had been by my side for nine years and I don't know how I can live without him. I ran outside, hoping he slipped out. I looked around, but no sign of him anywhere.

What am I going to do? Tears slid down my face unfettered. I tried to hold back, but I can't. I pick up my phone. I needed to talk to someone to calm myself down. "Maxum"

"Alli, what's wrong? You sound look you have been crying?"

"Finn is missing, and I don't know what to do?"

"I'm on my way. Don't worry, we will find him. Just wait for me."

Something about the way he spoke reassured me.

Chapter 16

Losing Finn forever would absolutely break me. I have had him since I was fifteen years old, and I always assumed he would be here forever. He literally has been my side for the good and the bad, the awkward teenage years, and everything else. I didn't have any siblings, but with Finn, I'm never alone. The fact that he just up and disappeared breaks my heart. I was racking my brain, thinking of where he could be.

"Thank you so much," I said, giving Maxum a side hug. "You didn't have to come."

"Of course, I had to come." He said. "And you don't need to thank me. I'm here because I want to be here. Where did you lose him?" He said, leaning against his car.

Having Maxum in my corner is really reassuring. "I don't know," I said. "I just came back, and he was gone."

"When was the last time you saw him?" He asked.

"Yesterday before I left for the party."

"Alright, don't worry. He probably didn't go far." He reassured me. "Follow me to my trunk. I have something that might help us find him." He opened his trunk. It's full of fliers with Finn's picture. They read 'IF YOU SEE THIS CAT. PLEASE CALL THIS NUMBER $1000 reward IF FOUND'.

I gasped. "Maxum. When did you have time to do all this?"

"I have a printer in my apartment, so I searched your Instagram to get a picture."

"Maxum, thank you I-"

He put his index finger to my lips. "Shhh, you don't need to say anything. Let's find your cat."

"But the $1000 reward is a bit.."

"Don't worry. I'm paying."

He doesn't have to do any of this, but here he is doing it all and more. "Thank you. I appreciate it more than words can say."

I grab fliers and tape. Maxum does the same. I'm going to find Finn, no matter what.

"Alli!" A voice echoed.

I turned around, and Jessica ran towards me. She pulled me into a hug. I reciprocated the hug. My anger at her dissipated as soon as I was in her arms. I just needed my best friend. Forget about the irrelevant stuff.

"I came here as soon as I heard ." she said. "I'm so sorry about leaving you yesterday. I shouldn't have done that. I was drunk."

"No, it's fine. I'm not angry with you anymore." I said.

Jessica has known Finn as long as I have, so she understands my pain more.

Maxum looked at us in amusement.

Jessica broke the hug. "Alright, let's go find him!"

"Here, take some of the fliers," Maxum said while passing them over.

"Oh, did you make the fliers?"

He nodded his head. "Yeah, I did."

"Wow, that's nice." She said, with a knowing smile. A look I had seen many times- you are gonna give me all the deets later look. She takes a look at the fliers while placing the rest in her bag. Her eyes flew open. "One Thousand Dollars?" Jessica and I have similar backgrounds, coming from middle-class families, everyone is always frugal with their money.

Max chuckled. "Yeah. It's to give people an incentive."

Jessica nodded her head. "Fifty bucks should have been enough. But hey, it's your choice. I don't have to chip in. Do I?" she whispered in my ear. "That's literally rent money." Her comment made me laugh.

"No, you don't. He is taking care of it." I whispered.

"Go, Maxum." She said, chuckling.

"What are you guys laughing about?"

"Nothing."

The next hour goes by fast, handing out fliers to anyone passing by and taping them on any available post. It is an exhausting process.

"Fuck I'm tired," Jessica said, breathing heavily.

"Same here," I said. "I just hope we find him."

"Don't worry; we will," Maxum said. "We still have a few more streets to cover. Maxum never seems tired. Here I am, about to pass out, and he is more ready than ever. His phone rang loudly. "Hello. Yes. Yes. I'm the one who put up the fliers."

Oh, My God. Did someone find Finn? I am anticipating the information.

"Alright, alright, I'll send you the address." He said. "Yes. And thank you so much; bye." He hung up and exhaled heavily.

"So?"

"Someone found Finn on the next street!!! She saw the flier."

"Oh my God!!!!"

"Amazing." Jessica shrieked.

I am just grateful. I'm so happy. This is the kind of good news I need:

******

"Thank you once again, Miss Sarah," I said. I'm so grateful to have Finn back. I crouched down to rub Finn's hair. He purred, touching my legs.

"You are welcome," she said. She looks like she is in her late fifties. She came to my apartment with Finn, her cat Princess, and the kittens. Apparently, I'm a grandma to fur babies!

"The kittens are so cute," Jessica said, gazing at them. "I didn't know you had it in you, Finn."

Everyone burst into laughter.

"Miss Sarah, here's a check for the reward," Maxum said with a small smile.

She shook her head. "No, son, I didn't do this for the reward. I just wanted to return the cat to his rightful owner."

She's nice. I know I wouldn't turn down such an amount.

"Well, I insist. You have a lot of kittens to care for. This will help with feeding them."

"That's nice of you, son, but I don't need it," she insisted.

"Please accept it," I said. "for the sake of the kittens."

"Yeah, please accept it," Jessica said.

She let out a deep breath. "Alright." She hugged Maxum and whispered, "Thank you."

"No problem," Maxum said. She deserved the reward money because of her kindness.

"So what are we going to do with the kittens?" I asked. "We

can take the ones you don't want to the shelter." I didn't feel like it was right for her to shoulder the responsibilities.

"That's a good idea," she said. "My granddaughter wants one. I'll let her choose before I take them in."

"Sounds like a plan." Jessica chimed in.

"Yeah, that sounds like a good plan. My friend runs a no-kill shelter. I'd be happy to call him." Maxum said.

"Finn," Miss Sarah said, crouching to rub his fur. "You are welcome to my home anytime." Finn happily purred. He must be really comfortable with her; he doesn't do that for everyone.

"Thank you, we will come to visit Princess after he's neutered," I said, chuckling.

"I would love to stay, but I'm gonna be late for bingo," Miss Sarah said.

"Alright, I will call my friend to see when you can drop the kittens off," Maxum said.

"Thanks again," I said. And with that, she walked out the door.

"Whew, I can't believe we found Finn," I said, pulling him in a hug. "I'm so happy." His touch is warm, and I feel safe in his arms. I don't want to move.

"Do you guys need a minute?" Jessica said, chuckling.

I honestly forgot Jessica was here. Both of us let go immediately. I coughed awkwardly.

"Well, now that's taken care of, why don't we celebrate?" Maxum said. "I heard about a drive-in screening of 'Titanic.' It'll be fun. I can call Simon to join in."

"Wow, that would be great," I said. "I'm in." A movie sounds great after all the turmoil plus; I haven't been to the movies in ages.

He gazed at me. "Yeah. It would be great. I'll check on the tickets. It's this evening."

"What do you think, Jessica? You have been quiet." I asked, tapping her shoulder.

"Actually, you guys go ahead. I have some stuff to do." She seems a bit off.

"It's fine, Jessica, if you're busy," Maxum said. "We're still on, right, Alli?"

"Yes. Let's do it!"

"Great. I'll be back." He disappears into my kitchen.

As soon as he is out of sight, Jess taps my shoulders. "I'll be waiting for details about your date later."

My eyes flew open. "This is not a date," I whispered.

"Yes, it is. And you'll definitely thank me later for leaving you guys alone. This ship needs to sail, finally."

My cheeks reddened. "Whatever."

Chapter 17

I know this might sound cheesy, but something I have always wanted to do is watch a movie with my boyfriend. It's on my bucket list. I know it sounds simple, but I have never experienced it, and I always wondered what that would feel like. I know Maxum, and I are just friends, but I can't deny there is something going on. There is a thin line between friendship and dating, and I'm hoping we crossed it. Watching a movie together at the drive-in is a test for both of us to see if there's something there.

It's time. I chose a simple purple mini-dress with heels. The Drive-in is filled with lots of cars. Night has fallen, and the light from the projector shined brightly. It is surreal. I guess people really do like drive-in movies.

I am in the passenger seat while Maxum is driving. He was trying to find a place to park. I see a parking spot close to the back of the lot and pointed him to it. Opening credits start as soon as we pull in. "We came right on time," he said with a small smile.

"Yeah, we made it," I replied. My heart is racing. I am trying to keep it together. The movie started with a Young Leo Di Caprio. I watched intently. Time passes, and there is nothing but silence between us. I focused on the movie. Maxum was unusually quiet. He just stared at the screen.

"You seem to really like the movie," he said, resting his hand on his chin.

"Yeah, I love titanic. I have watched it so many times"

"I'm glad. I wasn't sure you would come."

"Really? Why wouldn't I?"

"You seem like more of an introvert, and I wasn't sure if you like stuff like this."

I am an introvert, so he knows me better than I thought.

"Is that how I seem?"

"Yeah." He replied. "That's why I offered to bring Jessica and Simon along. I wanted you to be comfortable."

I don't know what to say. He is always so considerate. I can't believe he wanted to invite Simon and Jessica just to put me at ease.

"Wow, I don't know what to say. You are always looking out for me."

"Well, what can I say? I'm a good guy. To tell you the truth, I was a bit nervous when I asked."

He didn't seem like the kind of guy that gets nervous. He seemed so confident in himself.

"Why would you be nervous?"

"Because of you, silly."

"What? Why?"

He cleared his throat and turned to look me in the eyes. Not saying a word. The tension between us is thick. He cupped my chin with his right hand. His eyes are hooded, and I swear he looks like he could eat me alive! "When I saw you in that dress, you looked so beautiful, and the nerves kicked in. I thought I was going to say the wrong thing."

Wow. I didn't know I had such an effect on him. "You could never say the wrong thing to me."

He rubbed my lips with his thumb and leaned in slightly. "May I kiss you, Alexandra Hart?"

"Yes," I sighed.

He leaned in and kissed me. A wave of exhilaration washed over me. The kiss is better than I could imagine. It felt like fireworks going off in my head. So damn good. Amazing. So good that I wondered why I hadn't kissed him before. He deepened the kiss, his tongue delved into my mouth, and I gladly welcomed it. His taste is like heaven, and I couldn't get enough. His kiss was addictive. I felt a sensation all over my body, all the way to my toes. Making out in a car can be restrictive, but it's super hot. I don't know if it had been minutes or hours, but we just kissed, tasted, and touched, oblivious to the outside world. I groaned out of frustration when we had to come up for air.

"Fuck. Is that what I have been missing out on all this time." He said. He licked his lips.

"Right back at you. We wasted so much time."

"So much time."

"I know one thing."

"What's that?"

"I'm definitely doing that again and again."

He leaned in again and brushed his lips against mine. His lips are addictive. My hand caressed his chest as he placed a hand on my waist, pulling me closer. He pulled me across to straddle his lap, and my lady bits are singing. We are chest to chest while his tongue pushed into my mouth again, and I welcomed it. His blue eyes glistened in the night. His hands were everywhere, rubbing against the taut buds of my nipples and playing with the hem of my dress. I couldn't get enough of them. My hands tangled in his hair as he pulled me closer. We will definitely have to make up for the lost time. One thing I am sure of is there is no going back now. I'm addicted to him.

Maxum pulls back to look into my eyes. "We've got to stop now, baby, or I can't be responsible for how ends."

"Why? Who said I wanted it to end?" We're both breathing heavily, and I can tell from the solid ridge I feel beneath that he wants me just as much as I want him. "What if I don't want you to stop at all?" I lean for another kiss.

"Warrior, you're killing me. I want you so bad it hurts, but I will not make love to you for the first time in the front seat of my car and especially when there's the potential for a full audience."

I crawl away in embarrassment. "I'm sorry," I say as I duck my head in shame.

"No baby, don't say you're sorry. That was hot as fuck, and I plan to do it again and again." He begins to back out and says, "for sanity's sake, I think we better call it a night."

****

I drift off to sleep with visions of smoldering blue eyes and the memory of hot as fuck kisses. Sweetest dreams ever!

Chapter 18

Spending time with Jessica is very necessary after everything that happened. I needed to talk to someone about everything. Jessica's apartment wasn't too far away from mine, so I headed over there the very next day. We both sat on her couch. My mind was all over the place. I couldn't stop replaying yesterday's kiss in my mind. I touched my lips. What they say in movies is true. Even reminiscing about the kiss gives me goosebumps.

"So, how was the kiss?"

"It was amazing. It was everything I dreamed about and more."

She squealed. "OMG, I'm so glad you are finally getting some action."

I smacked her hand. "Whatever."

"So what happened after the kiss?" She asked, folding her arms together.

"We finished the movie, and he dropped me off at home."

"That's it? Boo."

"What else did you want to happen?" I said, chuckling. "Get your mind out of the gutter!"

She playfully hit my arm. "Listen, Alli. You need to be assertive in situations like this. Guys like girls who take charge."

"Oh. Is that what you did with Simon?"

Her cheeks reddened. "Shut up. Why are you switching topics?"

"No, I'm not, actually. I'm actually in the dark about you and Simon. You haven't told me what's going on with you." I have been curious about where Jessica and Simon stand. Her behavior has been a little suspicious, considering they both disappeared from the party. I'm sure something happened between the two of them.

"Well." She began. " Simon and I hooked up.."

I gasped. "Wow, Really? You kept me in the dark."

"No, girl, it isn't like that. Just so many things have been going on, especially when you lost Finn. I have been wanting to tell you."

"Alright, fine, you have a valid point there. So," I said. "Give me all the details."

"There's not much to say, actually. We were both really drunk, and it was really a spur-of-the-moment kinda thing. I was so surprised when I woke up the next morning and saw him in my bed."

"Wow. You dirty girl." I said, chuckling.

She covered her eyes with her palm. "Stop it. It's not funny"

"Why so gloomy? Aren't you guys exclusive yet?"

She shook her head. "Well, he never said explicitly that he wants me to be exclusive or for us to date at all, really. I mean, we've been out a few times but nothing next level, you know?"

I jerked my head. "Well, what did he say when he woke up?"

"He basically said last night was great and kissed me on the cheek. He didn't say much after that. He was in a hurry. He had to get to work. He said he would call me."

I didn't know Simon could act like that, but that was a total player move. "Well, that wasn't the classiest way to leave things," I muttered dryly.

"I know. Right now, I'm confused about his intentions.

"And what do you want?"

She let out a deep breath. "I honestly want to see how things go. I need clarity on where we stand."

"Well, there you go. Now you need to tell him that."

"Yeah, I think I will. Thanks." She giggled. "It's funny."

"What?"

"Now that you're all lovey-dovey with Maxum, you start giving relationship advice like a grownup."

We both howl in fits of laughter

******

Being an independent woman is something I have always had great pride in. I work hard, pay my bills, make my own money, and do whatever I want with it. I arrived right on time for my shift. As I walked in, Ian waved me over. "You have been coming to work on time lately. I wanted you to know I noticed," He said. "Good Job."

"Thank you."

"Hi, Alli," Rory said.

"Hey, Rory," I said. "How is your daughter? Are things better now?"

"Much better, thank you. She had a fever, and I was afraid to take her to daycare. She's back to normal, though."

"That's good."

"Thanks for covering my shift."

"You are welcome. Anything for the babies." We all chuckle

Some time passed, and quite a few customers started to trickle in.

"Alli, go attend table three," Ian yelled.

"Got it."

I walked quickly to the table of four. They all looked like college students.

"Hello, my name is Alli. Welcome to Forever Cafe. What can I get you?"

"I want an espresso."

" I want an espresso as well"

"I want a mocha latte."

"I want a cappuccino."

Sheesh! I scribble it down on my notepad. "Okay, that's two espressos, one mocha latte, and a cappuccino coming right up."

I handed the notepad to Rory since she was on drinks. I turned back, and to my surprise, Maxum walked in. Our eyes met as he walks in. He winks at me and takes his seat. I walk over to his table. I have to serve my customers. Right?

"Well, if it isn't my favorite customer."

"Well, if it isn't my favorite girl."

"What are you doing here? Do you really love the coffee that much, or can't get enough of my face?"

"You caught me. I can't get enough of your beautiful face," he said, smiling.

My cheeks burn. Everything seems so easy between us. I love how comfortable I am with him. "I knew it all the time," I say saucily.

He glanced at me intently. "What time do you get off?"

"I still have a few hours. Why?"

"I wanna take you somewhere."

My heart raced. We had already been on a date, and judging by how nice that date was. I am sure this will be a nice one as well.

"Really?"

"Yeah. Just change as soon as you get in, and I'll be by to pick you up around 6. Will that work?"

"Alright."

He immediately stood up from his chair.

My head jerked. "Aren't you ordering a coffee?"

He shook his head. "No, I wanted to see your face and deliver the message. Now that I've done that, I've got to head out."

I honestly thought stuff like this only happened in the movies. "What if I'd said no?"

"Then I would have had to kiss you into submission," he said, wiggling his brows.

"Damn" He laughed as he made his way to the exit

"Alli. Get to Table Five!" Ian said.

"I have to go, but I'll see you after work," I said, waving at him.

"see you then"

"Oh, wait. How should I dress?"

"Just be yourself, baby. That's all I need." He sauntered out the door, and I smiled all the way to table five.

Chapter 19

I'm a very impatient person, so going on a date when I have no idea where we are going is nerve-wracking, and I'm also pretty nervous. The wind blew through my hair as we traveled. Taylor Swift's wistful voice blared from the radio. We had been riding for a while now, and I am very curious about where we are going.

"So you are really not going to tell me where we are going?"

"Nope. It's a secret."

I clasped my hands nervously. "Okay."

"Relax. We are almost there."

I let out a deep breath. "Alright."

"Don't worry. You are gonna love it. I swear." He said, smiling. He drove steadily for some time. I glanced over, but he was concentrating on the road. We finally reached our destination. He parked the car and turned off the ignition. The house we're in front of looked amazing. It looked like a perfect summer house. I could see the beach from here.

"Where are we?"

"We are at my family's beach house."

I didn't want it to seem like a big deal. I shrugged. "Alright."

He opened the trunk and pulled out a picnic basket and a blanket.

"I'll hold the blanket," I said.

"Thank you, madam," he said with a bow.

"Yeah…."

"Well, let's go," he said excitedly. We walked hand in hand to the beach. The weather was perfect. There weren't a lot of people around. It was almost like our own private oasis. He removed his shoes as I lay out the blanket. He sat the basket atop and yelled: "Last one in is a rotten egg!!" He ran towards the waves.

I removed my shoes and ran after him. The competitive spirit fired inside me. He reached there first and put his feet in the shallows.

"I win!"

I hit his chest. "That's only because you cheated."

"Whatever, I still won." He said, chuckling.

"Whatever, indeed," I said, chuckling. We stand in silence for a while, just enjoying the silence as the water laps against us. "This is so nice."

"You know what? This moment needs to be captured." He said. He brought out his phone from his pocket. He stretched his phone for a selfie. I posed with a peace sign. I am not a fan of taking pictures, but I'm doing it for him. We played along the water's edge until hunger set in.

I sat down on the blanket, and Maxum sat beside me. He opened the basket and started to pull out the contents. It had all my favorite snacks: Oreos, sandwiches, chocolate, water, juice, and a very expensive bottle of wine and glasses. I'm a sucker for Oreos!!! "Dude. You thought of everything! You even got my favorite; Oreos! Thank you so much."

"You don't need to thank me." We ate in companionable silence while watching the waves.

"I really am enjoying myself, thank you."

"I'm just glad you are happy. I wanted today to be perfect for you."

"I don't know what to say."

"You are my girlfriend. Of course, I want everything to be perfect for you."

"Girlfriend?" This is the first time he's referred to me as his girlfriend. Of course, I know we are not platonic anymore, but it was never explicitly stated.

"Why do you sound so surprised?" He turned to look at me.

"Because you never said out loud that I am your girlfriend. I didn't wanna assume."

He clasped my hand. "I'm sorry. I thought it was obvious how I feel about you. Listen, I'm not here to play games. After we kissed, it solidified things. I like you, Alli, a lot. Truth is, I've had feelings for you almost since the day we met." He seemed so sincere and filled with emotions. It felt like the two of us were in our own world. I could feel my heart racing.

"I like you too, Maxum. A lot."

He leaned in and kissed me. His lips moved slowly, almost experimentally, before it intensified. His tongue swept into my mouth. My heart thumped so loudly that I was afraid he would hear it. His hand nestled on my waist while my hands are wrapped in his hair. His lips left mine. His eyes are filled with lust.

"Do you wanna get outta here?" He whispered in my ear.

I looked into his eyes and instantly knew what I wanted. "Yes."

That was all the response he needed. He didn't waste a minute. With the blanket and basket in one hand, he towed me into his house with the other. He held my hand as we walked into a bedroom. He pulled a condom from his wallet as we fell onto the bed. We rolled over several times, lost in the moment. My legs around his waist and his hands caressing my back. His lips are devouring mine. My heart thrummed in anticipation. He fisted my hair and deepened the kiss. I could feel his erection, and my panties are soaked.

He broke the kiss. "Fuck I have wanted this since the first day I saw you."

"From the very first day?"

"Yes, baby. Even when you were yelling at me, I thought you were sexy as hell."

"Wow."

"And now that I have you. I'm never letting you go."

I pulled his T-shirt up over his head and threw it to the floor, revealing his broad chest. He unzips my dress, leaving me in my bra and panties. He pulled off his pants and threw them on the floor, leaving him in his boxer briefs. And oh my! My heart raced, and I could feel the wetness between my thighs.

He kisses me again on the lips before trailing down my neck and my stomach.

I had to tell him now. We were getting so close to the finish line.

I broke the kiss. "Maxum. I need to tell you something."

"Yeah. Go on."

"I am a Virgin."

He looked surprised. "What? Really?"

I nod my head. "Yeah. I know that might be a turnoff for you.."

He shook his head. "Of course, it isn't. I'm just surprised. I'm definitely not turned off. If possible, it makes me want you more. You're perfect, and I want you. As long as you're sure."

I don't know what I expected, but that wasn't it. "I just wanted you to know."

"Listen, we don't have to do anything if you don't want to. We can take it slow."

"No, I want to. I want to be with you."

"Are you sure?"

"Yes, I'm sure." I am one hundred percent sure. I like Maxum so much, and I trust him to take care not to hurt me.

"I promise, baby. I'll be gentle." He kissed me intensely, pulling me closer to him. I feel in my heart that Maxum is the one for me.

The following morning, my eyes flew open. I was completely naked. Last night was amazing, and I couldn't stop replaying it in my head. My cheeks burned just thinking about it. The other side of the bed is empty. I put on his shirt and go to explore the rest of the house. I walked to the kitchen, and there Maxum stood making pancakes.

He smiled. "Good morning, babe."

"Good morning."

"You are finally up. I didn't want to wake you just yet. I wanted to get breakfast ready. How did you sleep?"

"Like a baby."

"Sit down and eat; breakfast is ready."

He placed pancakes on a plate and placed them in front of me. They are delicious.

"These pancakes are wonderful," I said in between bites and moans.

"Thank you. If you plan to finish, stop with the moans. They make me want something else" He came up and hugged me from behind, spooning me. I turned my head around, and he smiled at me.

How did I get so lucky? I thought. "What?"

He sat down next to me and held my hand. "I'm still thinking about last night," he said. "It was amazing. I'm just happy to be with you."

My cheeks reddened. "Yeah, I'm really happy with you too."

"It's funny."

"What is?"

"When you spilled coffee on me. Did you think we would be here right now?"

"No, but I'm happy we got here."

He had a devilish look in his eyes. I knew that look. His lips met mine again, "I think I'm going to need my shirt"

Finding love with Maxum was unexpected, but it is easy and comfortable. He is the best thing that ever happened to me, and I'm so grateful he came into my life. He's shown me what real love is. If I knew love would come to be by spilling coffee, I would have done it sooner.

Chapter 20

Six **Months Later.**

Today is my birthday. I don't celebrate birthdays, I always felt like celebrating it was a waste of money, and I didn't feel it was important in the grand scheme of things. My dad, of course, tried to celebrate my birthdays growing up. I didn't wanna make today a big deal, I wasn't gonna celebrate, but Max insisted.

We started the day out with me doing a photo shoot, of all things! I stood behind a white backdrop wearing a sleeveless red dress with matching heels. I hate taking pictures, and the flashes from the camera unnerved me but the things you do for love.

"Now smile for the camera." The photographer said.

My smile grew wider. "I can't believe you got me to agree to this."

"Well, I did have to beg," He said, chuckling.

"I came, so that has to count for something."

I do so many poses that I feel like a Kardashian by the time

I'm done.

Maxum looked on proudly. He gave me some thumb ups.

"Why don't you join your wife for a few shots?"

His wife???? Wait; what? Are we giving off married vibes? My eyes flew open, and my cheeks reddened. "We are not married."

Maxum coughed awkwardly. "Yeah, we are not married. She is my girlfriend."

The photographer looked amused. "Alright, why don't you join your girlfriend?

"C'mon, Maxum. Hurry up." I gestured.

"Alright, I'm coming." He walked over to where I stood and held my hands.

The flashes from the camera went off. "Lovely! Lovely! The pictures look so natural." The photographer said.

Maxum placed his hands on my hips, pulling me closer.

"Now, big smiles, and both of you say cheese."

"Cheese!"

****

Maxum is in the driver's seat while Maroon Five blasts through the speakers.

"I actually had more fun than I thought I would. Thank you, baby."

"It was my pleasure. I want you to be happy."

"So now that we are heading back to my place. You wanna Netflix and chill?"

He nodded his head. "Sure."

"Great. I'll make popcorn."

He pulled the car to a stop and hops out to help me. He's on my heels as I walk to the door. The swings open suddenly, and "Surprise!!!! Happy Birthday!" Everyone yelled simultaneously.

"Oh, My God!" I screamed while covering my face. I'm so surprised he was able to do this. My family and friends are here; Jessica, Simon, my dad, Rory, Ian, and Maxum's sister Linda. They are smiling ear to ear. I have never had a surprise party before, so I didn't suspect anything. Everywhere is decorated with balloons and streamers. ALLI'S BIG 25 is emblazoned on a banner. Jessica held a big pink cake with HAPPY BIRTHDAY ALLI written on it.

"Happy birthday, babe," Maxum said. He pulled me in for a hug.

I am so happy. I feel so loved. I said I don't celebrate birthdays, but I'm grateful for everything.

"Okay, love birds," Jessica said. "Let everyone else get a chance to talk to the birthday girl."

Maxum and I broke apart.

"Happy birthday, Bestie," Jess said.

"Thank you so much, babes.

"I know you are not a fan of birthdays or attention, but just enjoy yourself." She replied.

"Alright."

"Happy Birthday Alli!" Simon said. "I hope you enjoy your day."

"Thanks, Simon!"

Jessica and Simon went on a few more dates to see if there was anything more, but it ultimately fizzled out, and they decided to be friends. Of course, it was awkward at first, but they've gotten past it.

"Well, I guess my little girl isn't a little girl anymore," Dad said.

I wrapped my arms around his shoulder. "Aww, dad, I'll always be your little girl."

"Time really flies, doesn't it?" He said. "When Maxum called me up and said he is throwing a surprise birthday for you, I was surprised. I know you don't do birthday celebrations, but I'm so happy."

Maxum has met my dad numerous times, and Dad approves of our relationship wholeheartedly. They have a lot in common, so he finally has someone he can talk sports with.

"Wow, Maxum. You didn't need to do all this."

"I did it because I wanted to." He said, smiling. "I wanted you to enjoy your big day. That prompted a lot of awwws from everyone.

"Maxum. You really did a good job." Dad said.

"Thank you, Sir," he said, smiling.

"Well, C'mon, guys, let's get the party started!" Jessica exclaimed.

Food, drinks, fun, and mayhem ensued. There was pizza, beer, heavy hors d'oeuvres, and a full bar. Music blasted through the speakers.

Dad walked up to me with his lady. "So, Alli, there is someone I would like you to meet. This is Megan. Megan, my daughter, Alexandra."

I recognize her immediately because he has shown me her pictures and I have spoken to her on the phone. "Nice to finally meet you in person," I said, smiling. "I have heard so much about you."

She looks radiant. "I'm so glad to meet you too. Happy Birthday."

"Thank you, and I hope we see each other more often. Right, dad?"

"Yeah, Right, honey." He said, smiling. I'm happy if my dad is happy, and he seems really happy with her.

"Sorry to interrupt, but can I borrow the birthday girl? Is that okay?" Maxum said. He came out of nowhere.

"Yeah, of course," Dad said. "Go ahead." He grabbed my hand and whisked me away to my room.

"So, what's up?"

"I wanted to give your birthday gift in private." He falls to one knee. "You, my tiny warrior, are my heart's desire. I never thought I wanted love until I met you." Tears are streaming down my face, and I can't stop them. "I wanted to wait until after the party so that you could fully enjoy your day, but I couldn't wait."

"No, this is perfect. You, Maximilian Greyson, are the love of my life and my heart's desire. I don't want to go another day without you."

"So, will you do me the honor of becoming my wife til death do us part?"

"Absolutely!" We kissed passionately but soon had to break it off.

"You have guests," Maxum said. "We'll finish this later." I smiled as he slipped the biggest ring I'd ever seen onto my finger. "Let's make it quick," I said as we walked back into the living room.

Looking around. I felt so grateful. I feel an urgent need to give a speech. "Attention! Attention, everyone!" The room quieted as all eyes turned to me. "Hello, everyone, I'm not really good at giving speeches, but I'm gonna try. I want to thank everyone for coming today and celebrating my birthday with me, leaving your busy schedules, and honoring me with your presence. I'm really grateful to have people in my life that care about me so much, and I want to thank everyone. I don't know what I did to deserve this amount of support from all of you, but I love you all, and this is definitely the best birthday I ever had. Twenty Five never looked so good to me. Thank you so much once again."

There is a round of applause from everyone in the room. Dad is wiping away a tear, and so is Jessica. Maxum looked emotional.

"Babe, let's blow out your candles,' Maxum said. He walked over to me with the cake. The candle is lit with fire. I grabbed the cake and held on to it.

"Alright, honey, make a wish," Dad said.

I wish to be surrounded forever by the ones I love the most, my family and friends. I wish for happiness with Maxum. I blew out the candles. There is a sea of applause. Everyone clapped.

It's funny. My life now is so different than it was before. I have an amazing fiancee, friends, family, and a thriving work experience. Things are looking for me. We're blissfully on our way to becoming Mr. and Mrs. Greyson. I can hardly wait to see what the future has in store.

The End

About the Author

Lexi Richards is a talented author with a knack for creative writing. Her love for writing was borne out of the need to put down her limitless idea into a book in which readers could share her passion and delve into her realm. Lexi is a Human Resource Representative by profession who holds a Master's in Public Administration.

Lexi captures the readers' minds with her artistry and suspenseful writing that is simple, easily understandable, with a smooth flow and a great style that gets readers hooked on her book from the start till the end.

In her debut book *Chasing Max*, Lexi introduced the readers to Maxine, who is the protagonist in her story. She's brought you into the lives of Antoinette and Samantha as they found their happily ever afters (*Greyson Girls series*). Now step into the world of Maximilian and Alexandra and share the journey to *Becoming Greyson*.

You can connect with me on:

🌐 https://www.lexirichards.website

f https://www.facebook.com/profile.php?id=100086387727607

www.ingramcontent.com/pod-product-compliance
Lightning Source LLC
Chambersburg PA
CBHW071338130726
47996CB00002B/784